PICKUP MEN

L. C. CHASE

RIPTIDE PUBLISHING

Riptide Publishing
PO Box 6652
Hillsborough, NJ 08844
www.riptidepublishing.com

This is a work of fiction. Names, characters, places, and incidents are either the product of the author's imagination or are used fictitiously. Any resemblance to actual persons living or dead, business establishments, events, or locales is entirely coincidental.

Pickup Men (Pickup Men, #1)
Copyright © 2013 by L.C. Chase

Cover Art by L.C. Chase, lcchase.com/design.htm
Editor: Gordon Warnock
Layout: L.C. Chase, lcchase.com/design.htm

All rights reserved. No part of this book may be reproduced or transmitted in any form or by any means, electronic or mechanical, including photocopying, recording, or by any information storage and retrieval system without the written permission of the publisher, and where permitted by law. Reviewers may quote brief passages in a review. To request permission and all other inquiries, contact Riptide Publishing at the mailing address above, at Riptidepublishing.com, or at marketing@riptidepublishing.com.

ISBN: 978-1-62649-057-4

First edition
July, 2013

Also available in ebook:
ISBN: 978-1-62649-028-4

PICKUP MEN

L.C. CHASE

For the cowboys who inspire me.

TABLE OF CONTENTS

Chapter 1 1
Chapter 2 9
Chapter 3 15
Chapter 4 21
Chapter 5 33
Chapter 6 43
Chapter 7 53
Chapter 8 63
Chapter 9 75
Chapter 10 79
Chapter 11 87
Chapter 12 97
Chapter 13 105
Chapter 14 111
Chapter 15 119
Chapter 16 131
Epilogue 145

Chapter One

Two thousand pounds of pissed-off beef, aptly named Shockwave, tossed around the man on its back like a ragdoll. But Tripp wouldn't be dislodged. He clung to the spinning beast with an ease and confidence that belied the skill and athleticism—not to mention pure guts—required to compete at the professional level.

Sitting astride his best pickup horse, Fairgrave Flyer, near the chutes of the Santa Maria Elks Rodeo arena, Marty Fairgrave couldn't suppress the smile that fought for freedom across his face.

It was a beautiful sight watching a champion at work.

It was a beautiful sight watching Tripp Colby at the top of his game.

Marty's smile gained purchase as he recalled Tripp's firm, bare butt bouncing before him while Tripp had hopped around the small bedroom of Marty's travel trailer, pulling up his jeans and boots in a hurry to beat the rising sun earlier that morning.

The eight-second whistle blew, calling a clean end to Tripp's money ride and Marty's X-rated replay. Tripp dismounted Shockwave with enviable grace, landing upright but hard in the dirt. He stumbled forward a couple of steps before he got his center of gravity under him. It was textbook.

But as right as it was, it wasn't.

Marty's pickup partner, Bridge, pulled up beside him astride a stocky, bay gelding. "Where're the fucking stooges?"

Marty scanned the arena, registering every player in crisp detail. The hair on the back of his neck rose to attention. His smile snapped into a frown. An ice-cold finger trailed down his spine.

The two bullfighters were still dicking around, showboating for the audience at the opposite end of the ring. They should have been paying attention to their job. They should have jumped in to distract the bull from the vulnerable rider. Instead, they looked every bit the clueless rodeo clowns they were colorfully dressed as. This wasn't a fucking circus. And left alone, there was no way Tripp could reach the rails to get clear of the furious Shockwave, who had zeroed in on him like a missile.

There was no time to consider the consequences. No time to weigh the pros and cons, or proper protocols. Marty laid his boot heels to Fly's sides and raced out after Tripp. Ignoring Bridge's shout, he barreled into the path of what amounted to a runaway freight train.

Somewhere in the back of his mind, Marty knew what he was doing. Knew it was suicidal. It wasn't his job as a pickup man to pull a cowboy from a bull ride, let alone a bullfight. Bulls were too dangerous and unpredictable for them to sidle up to and sandwich between like the broncos. Marty's and Bridge's job was simply to haze the animal out of the arena as quickly as possible, before it could cause any damage. But right then, all he saw was Tripp lined up for a brutal ride on the ends of Shockwave's horns.

Not on my watch.

His pulse sped as time slowed in equal measure. His vision tunneled until all he saw was Tripp. All he heard was his own heartbeat and the pounding of Fly's hooves. He leaned in his saddle as he closed in, and held an arm out. Tripp grabbed on, his hand seizing Marty's forearm hard enough to bruise to the bone. Marty hauled Tripp off the ground and onto Fly's back, galloping clear of Shockwave. The heat of Tripp's body behind him, living and unharmed, was a heady comfort. A flash of black out of the corner of his eye told Marty how narrowly they'd escaped a horned broadside.

He pulled Fly up alongside the rails, and Tripp scrambled safely over the fence. Marty released a deep sigh of relief. Adrenaline still coursing through his veins, his muscles twitched as the panic released its hold. Turning his attention to Bridge, and the still-at-large bull, his lungs seized mid-exhale. Time froze in an intense, candid photograph—one of those "holy shit" moments that grace the centerfold of *National Geographic*. In this photograph, Shockwave bore down on him, too close. Bridge was right behind the bull, lasso suspended in the air mid-throw. The rodeo clowns—because they sure as hell weren't bullfighters—were blurred in the background, desperately running to catch up.

Time for reaction was over. The only thing left for him to do was pray.

Yeah, holy shit.

Marty heard a distant gasp ripple through the audience like a gale force. He braced himself, but it still took a long, profound second for him to realize it wasn't the wind bulldozing him and Fly into the unforgiving metal railing. It wasn't the wind that caused the surreal sensation of disembodiment as the ground rushed up to kiss him.

And it wasn't the wind that eclipsed the sun on a scream.

Thundering vibrations rumbled through the uneven earth beneath his back. Shadows flickered behind the red shades of his eyelids. Dust coated his throat and tickled his nose, and a light breeze carried mingling scents of leather, hot sweat, and livestock with it. Indistinguishable sounds teased his eardrums, rising and falling in pitch and volume and rhythm until they became definable. Concerned voices. Rapid hoofbeats. Braying cattle. Whinnying horses.

The last thing Marty remembered shot to the forefront of his mind and launched a scorching path of panic through his chest. His body tensed for flight, and his eyelids snapped open.

Pain came swift, sharp, and nauseating.

Blinding shards of unfiltered sunlight pierced his pupils and lanced straight through to the back of his skull. What felt like a thousand serrated knives stabbed mercilessly into his rib cage. He squeezed his eyes shut against the onslaught.

It hurt to breathe. It hurt to move. Hurt *not* to move.

Something large and solid hit the ground at his side with an *ooph*, quickly followed by a second, heavy thud. Rapid breaths puffed above him. Callused fingertips pressed against his neck, and a large hand gently brushed dirt from his face.

"Marty?" a deep, familiar voice pleaded. "C'mon, man."

Marty tempted the heavens again and cautiously lifted his eyelids. The lancing pain he feared didn't come. Bridge Sullivan and Kent Murphy—his best friends, practically brothers since grade school—were kneeling shoulder to shoulder at his side, their bodies forming a broad shield against the blinding sunlight. Equal parts worry and relief flashed in both pairs of eyes.

"You dumb son of a bitch." The soft tone of Bridge's deep voice belied the harsh words.

"What the fuck did you think you were doing?" Kent's voice was tight, like he was struggling to hold back either crying or yelling. "Jesus Christ, Marty. You know better."

Marty croaked out a rough, "I'm fine."

"The hell you are." Bridge pointed at Marty's head. "You're bleeding."

"You going to pass out?" Marty teased.

"Shut up."

Marty relaxed his eyes and feigned a smile. He couldn't be too bad off if Bridge wasn't heaving up his breakfast.

"How's Flyer?"

"You're fucking lucky, Smarts." Kent lifted his cowboy hat and wiped at the sweat on his forehead with his shirtsleeve. "Bridge roped Shockwave just before he hit you so you didn't get the full impact. Fly still got gored in the flank pretty good. It's not too deep, thanks to the angle you got nailed at, but he needs a ton of stitches."

"You won't be riding him anytime soon," Bridge added. "Won't be riding any horse for a while, by the looks of things."

"I'm fine." Marty pursed his lips. It was his job to keep the competitors from getting hurt, not to get hurt himself. "Just need a minute to get my bearings."

Kent shook his head. "Yeah, right."

Marty ignored Kent and turned his attention to the crowd that had gathered, scanning for one face in particular. The face that mattered most, the one that still made his heart skip a beat more than a year since the first time he'd laid eyes on it. Familiar, concerned faces stared back at him, but not the one he needed. In a low rasp he asked, "Where is he?"

Bridge and Kent both scowled at him and sat back on their heels. They could have been twins.

"Guys..."

With a reluctant sigh, Bridge tilted his head to the side. "Prick's standing back there."

Marty followed the direction of his friend's nod but still didn't see who he was looking for. His chest felt heavy, his head began to throb, and his bones ached. Flyer was one of his best pickup horses, and he'd put Fly's life—and his—in jeopardy. All because he'd fallen in love with a man who wouldn't— couldn't—acknowledge that he existed in public beyond the cursory post-rodeo thank-you.

Was he ever going to learn?

His breath caught sharply. There, at the outskirts of the small crowd, he found what he'd been searching for and locked onto a pair of piercing, light blue eyes.

Tripp stood with his hands buried in his pockets. His eyes were wide with fear and turmoil, lips pursed to a thin white line, body tense.

Please, Tripp.

With a determined expression on his handsome face, Tripp took a step forward. Paused. Then took another.

A cavalry of hope, bright and all-powerful, charged forward and forced the pain back into the shadows.

Tripp was actually coming to him. In public.

But just as Marty's heart began to swell, Tripp faltered to a stop, and his gaze broke away. His face instantly transformed into the practiced blank mask Marty had come to loathe. The cold shock of that broken moment punched a hole into his chest big enough to drive a semi through. Marty's internal army lost its hard-won ground, and every part of his body screamed in agony at its loss.

He closed his eyes and let the comforting earth suck him down.

"Move back, guys." The unfamiliar, authoritative voice with a sharp accent interrupted Marty's descent into oblivion. "Give the man some space here."

Two paramedics dropped down beside him, replacing his friends. One of the men began pulling the tools of their trade from a brightly colored medical bag, while the other gently straightened his neck and cradled his head so he couldn't move it. They efficiently went about assessing injuries and asking questions Marty wasn't really hearing.

He opened his mouth to tell them he was fine. He knew where he was, what had happened, his name, the day—even if his head was a bit fuzzy. He'd get up—in a minute—and get back to work, but the words stalled in the back of his throat when fingers pressed lightly against his right side, and sharp pain flared across his torso. He winced and hissed a shallow breath, and his vision grayed out briefly.

"Sorry." It was the paramedic with the accent. "No doubt you've got some broken ribs in there. We're going to have to..."

The man's voice faded as though it had been sucked up by some unseen vortex. He didn't care. He needed to see if Tripp was still there, and turned his head sideways in its loose hold.

Scott Gillard, the biggest homophobic prick on the circuit, was standing at Tripp's side. Scott laughed. Tripp smiled. Scott clapped Tripp on the shoulder, cast an impassive look at Marty, and walked away.

Tripp turned back to Marty. His shoulders slumped infinitesimally along with his mask. Feet rooted to the ground.

"Easy there." The paramedic who'd been holding his head strapped a c-collar around his neck to prevent him from moving again. "Let's make sure everything works before you go ripping up the dance floor, okay, cowboy?"

Marty would have laughed at the attempted levity any other time, but right now all he felt was an agonizing rawness clawing out his insides. He understood now, but that didn't make it hurt any less. Didn't make what had to happen any easier.

His heart seized mid-beat and splintered in his chest. Or maybe that was broken bone digging into flesh. Either way, the result was the same.

He barely registered Bridge telling him that he and Kent would meet him at the hospital, or the oxygen mask that had been secured over his mouth, or the hands that slid under his body and carefully rolled him onto his side to work a hard backboard under him. Straps tightened over his chest and legs, foam blocks immobilized his head, and cold bit into his back.

But it didn't matter.

He stared up at the spotless blue sky, drifting on the sensation of weightlessness for a brief moment when the paramedics lifted and settled him onto a gurney and then rolled him into the waiting ambulance.

A face edged into his blurring line of vision, words were spoken in a calming tone, but none of it registered. He closed his eyes and burned the last image of Tripp into his memory: the lean, defined frame of Tripp's body, the strong curve of a jaw shadowed with day-old stubble, the slight bend and bump in the bridge of a nose that had been broken more than once. The full, pink lips that had kissed him so passionately, bright eyes that had stared at him with heated desire, and jet-black hair that felt like silk sliding through his fingers. The mental keepsake would be all he'd have after today.

The ambulance doors closed resoundingly on Tripp, on their relationship, and on Marty's heart. Warm liquid slithered down his temple, and he vowed that would be the only tear he'd shed. Darkness wrapped around him, pushing out sound and thought, and blessedly, the pain of broken bones and shattered dreams.

Chapter Two

Thwaaap. Swoosh.

The shuffling sound of thin plastic was familiar, but it didn't fit with the last thing Marty remembered—laying on his back, body broken and heart breaking. Nor did it fit with the chemical bouquet of disinfectant, medication, and food that tainted the stale, dry air. He knew that smell all too well. In his line of business, the hospital was a regular destination—though generally not for himself. He felt responsible for every single cowboy who'd suffered injury on his watch and made a point of visiting each one in the hospital before heading off to the next stop on the circuit.

Thwaaap. Swoosh.

Marty lifted drug-heavy eyelids and stared at pocked ceiling tiles overhead while his vision defogged. He tried to swallow but couldn't form enough saliva to dislodge the lump from his throat or the tongue glued to the roof of his mouth. As his periphery cleared and sharpened, he surveyed the surroundings. Soft light from a small lamp on a bedside table cast tall shadows on bare, pale green walls. The door was slightly ajar; subdued activity and the murmur of voices drifted in from the hallway. The black of a moonless night hung like a drawn blind behind the matte glass of a wall-to-wall window.

Thwaaap. Swoosh.

He turned his head toward the source of the sound, and a dull ache throbbed in his temple, shoulder . . . whole body.

Bridge and Kent were sitting across from each other at a small table pushed up against the wall opposite the window. Expressions distracted, but attention rapt on the deck of playing cards Kent was deftly shuffling. Kent's blond hair was cropped short, but somehow managed to look messier than Bridge's, slightly too long and hanging in wind-blown disarray over his eyes.

They were both beautiful men. Good men. And they stood by him no matter how fierce the storm. They'd been the first people he'd told that he thought he was gay when he was thirteen. They'd shrugged their shoulders, said whatever, everyone already knew, and then asked if he was ready to go fishing. Apparently Marty had been the last to know, and that had earned him the nickname Smarts—for his lack thereof.

"So . . . I'm going to . . . live then?" His voice was a rough grate across dry vocal chords.

Two blond heads jerked up. Though starkly different faces—Bridge rugged with a Superman jawline and Kent with classically aristocratic angles—their relieved expressions were identical. Tension that had etched sharp lines around their mouths and eyes relaxed. Kent dropped the cards to the table, the game forgotten, as he and Bridge stood and walked over to Marty's bedside.

"Yeah, dumbass." Bridge crossed his arms and smiled. "And I hope that bull knocked some sense into your thick skull."

"You're definitely going to have some sense up there after I get done kicking your sorry ass," Kent said.

"Water?"

Kent reached for a covered plastic cup with a bendy straw sticking out and held it to Marty's lips. Marty sucked back three greedy gulps. He closed his eyes and followed the refreshing path it cut as it raced from his dust-encrusted mouth and down his parched throat to pool in the bottom of his empty stomach.

"Better?"

He opened his eyes and released the straw. "Yes, thank you."

Kent nodded and returned the cup to the bedside table.

"What time is it?" Not the first question Marty wanted to ask, but the other didn't matter anymore.

Kent watched him closely. "Visiting hours are almost over."

It doesn't matter. Marty tried to school his thoughts before they charged to the surface, but his friends knew him too well.

Even if he weren't foggy from painkillers, he wouldn't have been able to fool them.

Bridge shoved his hands into his back pockets. "He didn't come."

Marty knew Tripp wouldn't have, but still, that small kernel of hope that refused to be dislodged clung to the back of his mind and struggled to grow.

Kent shook his head. "Shit, Marty. I can't believe you did that. Damn near got yourself killed for that yellow son of a bitch."

"Pretty sure all my parts are still attached."

"That's not the point, Sergeant Sarcasm. You wouldn't have done that for someone like Scott Gillard."

"Oh, but I did. Remember?" Marty attempted to sit up, but a spike of pain curbed that idea before he'd even lifted his head and stole the heat from his voice. "You know that's why he doesn't hassle me."

"Yeah, but he wasn't riding a bull, and you weren't in love with him."

Way to suck the wind from my sails, Kent. Marty closed his eyes. A heavy wave of fatigue washed over him and pressed his body deeper into the thin mattress. He was tired of the same old argument. If only there was never any reason for it.

"He just fucking stood there, Marty. Like a damn deer caught in the headlights," Bridge said. No pity in his voice, no judgment, just fact. "None of us knew how bad off you were then. What if you were dying? What if that was the last—"

"Christ, guys! Give it a rest. Okay?" Marty immediately regretted the force of his words. Nausea chased the sharp knife blade that sliced over his rib cage. He squeezed his eyes shut and willed back the bile creeping up his throat. When the pain ebbed and his body settled back into its chemically induced numbness, he no longer had the energy in him to fight. They didn't know Tripp like he did. No one knew the real Tripp Colby. "He's got his reasons, and they're valid. Just leave it."

"Valid enough to leave you dying in the dirt? What kind of asshole does that?" Bridge's voice rose slightly. "And you still stand up for him?"

Marty huffed. "Dramatic, much?"

"Well—"

"Well, let it go. You guys win. I'm done being Tripp Colby's dirty little secret."

They exchanged a look Marty didn't have to see to know was a mix of surprise and approval. Kent turned to him and smirked. "It's about fucking time."

Marty had no idea what the look he shot his friends said, but he felt the red haze of anger it lashed out on. The smirk slid off Kent's face, and both of them looked down, finding something interesting on the floor to stare at. The squeaky wheel of a wheelchair or cart echoed down the hallway beyond Marty's room. Hushed voices rose and fell. Someone laughed.

Bridge shifted on his feet and looked up, his expression contrite. "It's not about winning, Marty. We just want what's best for you. Want you happy. You know that."

"I was happy with Tripp." *Mostly*.

"In secret," Kent said. "That's not right."

"Yeah, well. That's not an issue anymore." Marty's voice sounded as weak to his ears as it felt crawling over his tongue. "It's over."

Bridge and Kent were right. Always had been. He deserved someone who was out and *proud* to be seen with him, who *wanted* to be seen with him. But getting over Tripp wasn't going to be quick or easy. It wasn't like love came with an on/off switch.

Fatigue wrapped around him like a thick wool blanket, making his brain sluggish and muddy. He just wanted to sleep. Forget everything.

Kent cleared his throat. "We'll break you out tomorrow and drive you and your horses home."

The subject of Tripp Colby closed.

"Hesparia is next weekend. And I don't need to be driven anywhere," Marty grumbled.

"Right." Kent smiled, his smooth voice lighter. "No one wants to see you back in the saddle until the Folsom rodeo, and you can't drive with a fresh concussion."

"So be a good boy and stay home for a couple weeks." Bridge gathered up the deck of cards and their cowboy hats. "Enjoy your mama's cooking. Okay?"

"Okay."

"Good." Bridge walked back and handed one hat and the deck of cards to Kent. "All right then, we'll see you in the mornin.'"

Kent settled his hat on his head and dropped the cards onto Marty's bedside table. "Later, Smarts."

Marty was pretty sure he nodded, but his eyelids began to slide down against his will, and bright blue eyes followed him into darkness.

Chapter Three

He'd fucked up but good this time. Monumentally.

How he was going to make amends was the billion-dollar question.

Tripp sat in a relatively comfortable chair in the corner of the darkened hospital room, watching the steady rise and fall of Marty's chest. He looked so young lying there, more vulnerable than a man his size should. He was only a couple inches taller than Tripp's six feet, but he was solid. Somewhere between the brick house that was Bridge Sullivan and the lean runner's frame of Kent Murphy.

Tripp had heard of Marty—the gay pickup man, as the circuit locals called him—long before he'd actually seen the man at a rodeo in Salinas. When he finally did, he'd been mesmerized. It was more than Marty's looks, more than his unassuming strength and quick, easy smile—that unnamable "it" factor buckle bunnies and men alike noticed. No, there was so much more to Marty. He was one of those cowboys with a calling. He seemed somehow tuned in to the mysterious wavelengths of bucking horses and bulls and had an uncanny sense of knowing exactly where to be at exactly the right time.

For the rest of his days, Tripp would never forget the image of Flyer being slammed into the rails with Marty on his back. More than that, he'd never forget the pain in Marty's eyes as the ambulance doors closed. A pain beyond physical that Tripp knew he had caused all on his own.

A cold tremor rattled his body. His stomach roiled.

Tripp cursed under his breath and leaned forward to rest his elbows on his knees, dropping his head into his hands. Marty had put his life on the line without hesitation, had been willing to take the horns for him. And what did he do? Nothing. Not a goddamned thing.

What the fuck is wrong with me?

He should have gone to Marty. Wrapped his hands around Marty's and held tight. Made sure he was okay, made sure he knew Tripp was there for him and always would be. At least that's what he told himself he would have done.

If Scott hadn't come over.

If the demon he'd lived with all his life hadn't reared its ugly head.

But Scott had come over, and Tripp had given into the fear like he always did and played it straight. The only reason he'd befriended Scott in the first place was because he'd learned early on in life that it was the safest place to be—the sheep in wolf's clothing, hidden in plain sight. It was a strategy he'd mastered through years of experience by fears so deeply ingrained they'd held him back from giving the only person he'd ever cared for what was needed, deserved.

And people thought bull riders were courageous.

"Fuck." A short, mocking huff of a laugh escaped his mouth. How was he ever going to make up for this? He knew the answer to that, didn't he? There was only one thing he could do, but just the thought made him break out in a cold sweat. Hoof beats echoed in the back of his mind and sent his stomach on another nauseating spiral.

A low groan yanked him from his thoughts. He looked up, and his body tensed. Marty's eyes were open, staring unfocused at the ceiling. Tripp stood, drawing Marty's attention when he took off his hat and dropped it to the chair behind him.

"Hey, babe." Tripp stepped forward. He threaded his fingers through Marty's sun-streaked hair and leaned down to kiss his forehead. Marty's skin was a shade too warm. "How are you feeling?"

"Doc says I've got three busted ribs, a dislocated shoulder, and a concussion," Marty said, his voice low and sleep-rough. "And my mouth feels like the Mojave Desert."

Tripp reached for a white plastic cup on the bedside table and filled it with water from a jug sitting beside it. He snapped on the lid and shoved a straw through the hole, then held it to Marty's lips. Marty scowled and took the cup from him. A thread of unease snaked into Tripp's chest at the very un-Marty-like gesture.

After taking a few sips, Marty handed the cup back to Tripp without meeting his eyes. "What time is it?"

"Almost midnight."

"You snuck in?"

Tripp offered a halfhearted smile and took Marty's hand in his. "Yeah. I got here as soon as I could."

A weak *huff* escaped Marty's mouth. "Don't you mean as soon as you knew no one would see you?"

"Marty, please. Can we not start that right now? I've been going crazy worrying about you."

Marty lifted his gaze. Those beautiful gold-hazel eyes, normally dancing with warmth and open admiration, were flat and unreadable. Goose bumps broke out over Tripp's skin. Marty looked away and slowly, deliberately, pulled his hand free.

"Yeah, I could see how worried you were."

"What's that supposed to mean?" Tripp couldn't help the shake in his voice.

Marty glared, the bite in his tone unnerving. "What do you think it means?"

"There was a huge crowd around you." Tripp ran a hand through his hair. "I can't just turn off thirty-three years of thinking like a light switch. You know that."

"Jesus Christ, Tripp! Asking if I was—" Marty winced and sucked in a sharp breath, his complexion paling. Tripp reached out, but Marty waved him off as though he were swatting away a fly. He snapped uncharacteristically hard eyes back to Tripp, his voice reedy but still biting. "Asking if I was okay or maybe saying 'thank you for saving my life' might have been nice. What's so fucking suspicious about that?"

Tripp recoiled. Guilt, a bitter taste in the back of his throat, threatened to choke him. He couldn't form a reply. His gentle

Marty had never once raised his voice in anger as long as Tripp had known him.

You did this. That condescending voice in the back of his mind perked up. *Face it. You're no good for him.*

No. I can be. I will be.

"And what about Bridge and Kent? They're fucking straight, and no one ever questions our friendship as just that."

"It's not the same."

"Really? How so?"

"I'm a three-time world professional bull riding champion. My biggest sponsor would drop me faster than a greased pig. That's how. Kent's just a state champion steer wrestler, and Bridge is just a pickup man that no one ev—"

Fuck. Me. Tripp wanted to punch himself in the nose. Reel those last few words back in and burn them, but it was too late. They'd already found their mark. Raw pain shot through Marty's eyes, but he rebounded quickly and blanked his expression, retreated behind a wall Tripp had never seen before, never knew Marty had it in him to even erect. His pulse began to hammer.

"Shit, Marty. I didn't mean—"

"I know what you meant." The resigned, flat tone sent a ripple of panic through Tripp's veins. "I'm an arena ghost. No one notices the pickup men, and you're too high-profile to be seen with the infamous gay-and-out one. God forbid Jackson Motors should find out."

"That's not—"

"Save it." The fight was gone from Marty's voice, which Tripp found scarier than the anger. At least anger meant Marty felt something. "I can't do this anymore. I love you, Tripp. I do. But I can't do this."

"Marty..."

Marty shook his head. "I don't belong in your closet. Not in anyone's closet."

"Look, I fucked up today. I know it." Tripp wanted to reach out, run his fingers through Marty's hair, hold him. But fearing the reception, he kept his hands at his side. "Just give me a chance to make it up to you, babe." He knew it sounded like begging, but that was the least of his worries at the moment. Marty was the only good thing in his life—the only person he didn't have to wear his heavy, suffocating armor around, the only person who could keep the demons at bay.

Marty stared up at him, thinking, weighing. His flat, broken gaze began to shine with tears. "We're done, Tripp."

All the oxygen in the room sucked out and ripped from his lungs.

"Marty, I—" *love you.* The words lodged in the back of his throat. *God dammit! Say it, asshole!*

"Don't. Please." Marty closed his eyes. "Just go."

Tripp stared down at Marty as his brain stuttered to a flatline. Marty wouldn't open his eyes again, wouldn't look at him. And Tripp couldn't move, couldn't pull away.

He stood there frozen until Marty's breathing deepened and his body slackened. Tripp leaned down and kissed warm, soft lips that he would never get enough of and might never again. Not unless he grew some Shockwave-sized balls and did something about it. He brushed a hank of hair back from Marty's forehead and traced a finger along the wet path of a single tear that had carved down the side of his cheek.

"I'm not losing you, Martin Fairgrave." The vow was delivered in a hoarse whisper.

He swallowed a painful breath and turned to leave, to figure out how to make this right. Just as he reached the door—

"Tripp."

Oh, thank God! Relief nearly dropped him to his knees. He turned back and rushed toward Marty. But the next words stopped him dead in his tracks.

"Don't forget your hat."

Chapter Four

"Seriously, Marty."

"Seriously, Bridge." Marty leaned against the edge of the hospital bed and shoved his left foot into his boot with enough force to tweak his ribs, while Bridge and Kent looked on with raised eyebrows. He didn't do invalid well, and the last thing he wanted to do was ask his friends to put his boots on for him. Didn't matter that he couldn't use both hands to pull on the bootstraps, not with one arm being in a sling and all. "I can drive myself home."

"No, you can't." Kent stood at the end of the bed, the corner of his mouth tipped up in the start of a smile. At least he wasn't laughing at him. Yet. His lean arms were crossed over his chest, but Marty knew if he listed even a fraction of an inch, Kent would be right there to prevent him from falling.

Marty also knew arguing was a losing battle, especially when the two of them teamed up against him. If he were honest with himself, he really didn't have the energy to argue anyway. And if it were one of them who'd been injured, he wouldn't let them drive home alone either.

"Fine." He huffed and stepped into his right boot with a little more care. "But you both don't need to drive me. It's more than seven hours, and you"—he pointed at Kent—"have to be in Hesperia in a couple of days."

"Which only goes to show how bad you banged your head." Bridge stood at the other end of the bed mirroring Kent's posture. Blond bookends. "If Kent doesn't come too, how do you propose I get myself back after I drop off you *and* your truck?"

"My dad will drive you back."

Bridge snorted. "Have you forgotten what time of year it is, Smarts? Your dad's swamped on the ranch right now."

"Oh."

"Yeah, *oh*."

Marty frowned. Fairgrave Ranch was not only a family legacy but a successful working-guest ranch. It was a full-time business year-round, but at the height of tourist season, all hands were needed on deck.

No, Marty couldn't ask his dad, or anyone else for that matter, to drive Bridge all the way back down to Hesperia. That was a ten-hour round trip, and no one on the ranch had the time to take a full day off. Marty forced back a little pang of guilt. His parents had insisted he got out and saw some of the country on the rodeo circuit. He was young, and they wanted him to kick up his heels a little, hopefully find someone to love before his dad handed the legacy down and the ranch became his life—for the rest of his life.

A soft but solid knock on the doorframe to the hospital room drew Marty's attention. The man standing there looked vaguely familiar, but Marty couldn't place where he may have seen him. He was wearing a lightweight athletic jacket over a tight-fitting white T-shirt that didn't hide a washboard stomach, faded jeans, and running shoes. Even from across the room, Marty noticed that the man's eyes were an unusual shade of violet.

"Hi. Sorry to interrupt." His voice had a heavy resonance and quick cadence. A New Yorker. Recognition clicked in Marty's mind as the man stepped a couple of feet into the room and extended his arm toward Marty. "I'm Eric. Eric Palmer. I was one of the EMTs on scene at the rodeo yesterday."

Marty's dominant hand was restrained tight to his chest in the sling, but he stepped forward and gave Eric's hand a clumsy shake with his left. "Thank you for looking after me out there."

"Just doing my job." Eric gave a slight nod. "I hope you don't mind, but I just wanted to drop by and see how you're doing. I like to see the people I bring in leave the hospital on their own two feet."

Bridge pushed away from the bed to stand beside Marty. "Ornery SOB is how he's doing."

"And his brains are still in the mixer," Kent said.

Eric chuckled.

"Pardon the dynamic duo." Marty sighed. "This is—"

"Bridge Sullivan and Kent Murphy." Eric stepped forward to shake their hands. "Pickup man and steer roper extraordinaire. It's a pleasure to meet you both."

Kent inclined his head, but Bridge wore an odd look that Marty couldn't identify, which was strange considering he'd known Bridge his whole life and could have sworn he knew every single expression possible and exactly what each one meant.

After what seemed like a lingering glance at Bridge, Eric turned to Marty with a hint of a smile. His gaze quickly raked over Marty with a barely perceptible pause at his crotch. The slow creep of heat through Marty's veins might have been the drugs or it might have been the result of Eric's confident perusal, but either way he decided to take it for what it was: simply a pleasant feeling.

"So they're letting you out," Eric said, and Marty decided he liked the sound of Eric's accent. It was . . . refreshing in a way he didn't think it could be. Probably because he was so used to the slower, laid-back West Coast accent and the southern drawls common on the rodeo circuit. There weren't a lot of New York cowboys this side of the divide.

"Yeah, but these yahoos won't listen to me when I say I don't need them to drive me home, and I most certainly don't need them both to. Kent has a roping clinic to run before the Hesperia rodeo this weekend, so he really needs to head straight there."

"And this jackass doesn't seem to understand he's not even allowed to drive right now." Bridge's tone was playful, and the odd expression on his face had vanished. Marty figured he must have imagined it, what with the painkillers and all.

"They're right, you can't drive yet," Eric said. "Whereabouts is home?"

Marty reached for his cowboy hat on the bed. "Bridgeport. Almost on the Nevada border."

Eric took on a calculated look. "Well, if you're all amenable, I have to be in Santa Clarita for a training course this weekend. Since it's roughly in the neighborhood, I'd be happy to follow along and then drop Bridge off."

Pregnant silence filled the room as Marty and his friends processed what Eric had just offered. While not entirely unheard of for a stranger to make such a grand gesture, it was certainly not all that common these days.

Marty spoke first. "I can't ask you that."

"You're not asking. I can take over for Kent so he gets to his clinic, you get safely home, and Bridge gets back to the rodeo in time. Everyone's covered. Just call it extended EMT services."

Bridge cleared his throat. "That's actually a good idea. I'm in."

Marty and Kent both turned to look at Bridge who, strangely, blushed. "What? It is a good idea."

Marty met Kent's gaze, and when Kent shrugged, Marty turned back to Eric. "Okay then. Thank you."

"Anytime."

"Well, then." Marty placed his hat onto his head and smiled. "Let's get the hell outta Dodge, boys."

Darkness had fully settled over the mountains and flooded the valley by the time they crossed the tall gates of Fairgrave Ranch and bounced down the long, dirt drive to the main house. Warm light spilled out through the lower level windows like a guiding beacon, and tiny lights from the occupied cabins beyond flickered in the distance like earthbound stars. Bridge steered Marty's Ford Super Duty past the house toward the owner's stables, and the halogen headlights splashed across the white sideboards of the large house, creating a soft, blue-white halo around it. Other than interior renovations and modernizing, the house was exactly as it had been when it was originally built, save for fresh coats of paint over the years, which never seemed to stray from the same stark white.

A second splash of light illuminated the house from the headlights of Eric's pickup truck. Eric pulled up beside Marty's rig and stepped out of his vehicle.

"May as well grab your gear." Marty slammed the passenger door and walked around to meet Eric. "It's too late for you guys to head out now, and there is no way my parents will let you leave before morning."

"Oh, I don't want to impose." Eric's breath pillowed out in a soft cloud that momentarily obscured his face. He shuddered as he spoke. "I can just camp out here."

"Ha!" Bridge walked around to the back of Marty's trailer to open the doors and start unloading the horses. "Good luck with that."

"What?" Eric reached into his truck to pull on a jacket and zip it up to his chin.

Bridge's voice carried through the open windows of the horse trailer. "You'll see."

Marty laughed at Eric's bewildered expression. "My parents. The second you walk through that front door, you're family. They won't allow you to rough it out here when there are perfectly good guest rooms in the house. Plus, it's only May, and we're over six thousand feet elevation here, which means it still dips down to freezing at night. My mom would never hear of it."

"Oh." Eric's voice was quiet, and for a second Marty thought he looked uncertain about the idea. He cleared his throat. "Well, if you're sure, I guess. I really don't mind staying out here."

"Don't worry, man." Bridge came around the trailer with Flyer in hand. He gave Eric a mock punch in the shoulder as he passed, leading Flyer slowly into the barn. "They'll love you."

They made quick work of unloading the horses and settling them in for the night, making sure Flyer's wounds were clean and redressed. Well, Bridge and Eric did. Neither of them would let Marty do a single thing, and having Eric back Bridge up with solid medical reasons why he needed to stay out of the way wasn't earning the man any brownie points in Marty's book. He even had to ask Eric to put his gloves on for him because he couldn't manage to get the left one on with his useless right hand. It was that or deal with the Wrath of Mother for getting frostbite because he'd been too proud to ask for help.

The three of them crossed the yard toward the house, Bridge carrying Marty's gear as well as his own, and before they even reached the first step of the wraparound veranda, the front door swung open and Ruth Fairgrave rushed out. Her hands fluttered around Marty for a moment, as if unsure where she could touch him without hurting him. She finally settled on reaching up to cup his face, pulling him down for a kiss on the cheek.

"I can half hug," he said. "Just be careful of my right side."

He tucked her into his uninjured side, and she rested her head briefly against his chest. Then she tilted her head back to look up at him with soft eyes the same green-hazel as his. "I'm so glad you're home, sweetheart."

"Sorry it's not for a better reason, Ma." He'd been on the road for two months, since the start of rodeo season, but his mom looked exactly the same as always. Healthy and eternally happy.

"Well, I won't disagree I'd rather have you here healthy, but any time you're here is good with me."

She gave him a squeeze around the waist before releasing him, then moved past him to throw her arms around Bridge. "Thank you for bringing my boy home."

"Anytime, Ruthie. I'm just glad I don't have to listen to him bitching and moaning anymore."

She stepped back and mock-swatted Bridge on the arm, then looked over at Eric. "And who might this handsome young man be?"

"Eric Palmer, ma'am. I was the EMT on scene yesterday."

He extended his hand, but Ruth swatted it out of the way and pulled him into a hug. Yes, his mom was a hugger. Best people just accepted that and let her have her way. Eric looked up and met Marty's eyes with something like shock. Maybe even a touch of apprehension, which made Marty wonder what Eric's life had been like up to this point.

"It's a pleasure to meet you. And please, call me Ruth. I'm too young to be a ma'am." She winked, and Eric, regaining his composure, laughed. "Thank you for taking care of my boy out there and escorting him home."

"Just doing my job, ma—Ruth."

"I didn't know home delivery was part of the service." All heads turned in the direction of the front door at the deep, gruff voice. Marty's bear of a dad stood just inside the foyer, cutting an imposing figure.

Eric shifted on his feet, the apprehension creeping back into his expression. "No, sir. Just helping out."

Again Marty wondered about Eric's past, why he seemed so nervous, and then cast another look at his dad. Okay, he was a big man, taller than Marty, with thick muscles earned by working the land and livestock. His face told a tale of hard-lived years in fine grooves around gray eyes that saw more than he let on, so Marty could see how that could be scary. Maybe. But his dad's mouth was always set in a hint of a smile, capped by a classic handlebar mustache trimmed just shy of obnoxious, which surely had to put people at ease.

His dad nodded. "Well, come on in then, boys. Ruthie's got dinner waiting on y'all, and I ain't about to freeze my balls off standing out here jawing." Marty stepped up over the threshold, and his dad gave him a quick, careful hug. "Good to see you, son."

He turned to smack Bridge playfully on the back. "Behaving yourself, Bridger?"

"You know it, buckaroo." Bridge grinned, and the light in his eyes danced.

His dad just shook his head, and when Eric reached the threshold, he struck out his hand. "Pleasure to make your acquaintance, Eric. If you know what's good for you, you'll call me by my given name, Buck. I ain't no *sir*."

"Will do." Eric stepped inside, and Buck closed the door behind them.

Two hours later, after they'd eaten a hearty, home-cooked meal and everyone had been assigned sleeping quarters and parted ways for the night, Marty was settling into his old bedroom when his mom walked in.

"What else is going on with you, sweetheart?" She sat down on the edge of the bed and looked up at him. "There's more pain in your eyes than there are injuries in your body."

Marty sighed and sat down beside her gingerly, making sure to keep her on his uninjured side. His family had always been close, and there wasn't much they didn't share with each other. And where his mom was concerned, there wasn't much she didn't seem to magically know already, anyway. "I broke it off with Tripp."

"Oh, honey." She reached for his hand and clasped it between hers. "But you love him."

"I do, but it's not enough. I can't live the way he lives. I don't know how. I've tried, but it's killing me."

"Couldn't you have found a way to work things out? Every relationship comes with a degree of compromise."

Marty shook his head. There was only one way it could work out, and it wasn't his place to demand it. "It should be equal give-and-take, shouldn't it?"

She nodded but didn't say anything.

"He's thirty-three years old, Ma, and I don't think he's ever coming out. At the rodeo yesterday he just stood back. Never came up to make sure I was okay, and then he snuck into the hospital after hours. There's no future for us. Not that way."

His mom frowned. "That's not like you to lose hope. And at his age, Tripp only has a couple of good years of bull riding left in him before he'll have to hang up his spurs."

"So we keep sneaking around and hiding what we are to each other? Hoping no one discovers we're together for two more years? And then what? He'll still be a celebrity in the PBR world. Besides, more than that holds him back. He won't tell me the details, but I know he didn't luck out like I did with such a great family."

"A good family should never be the luck of the draw, honey." She leaned into his shoulder, and he rested his chin on her head while they sat in silence. No matter what she said, he knew he'd lucked out, not only with his family but with his friends too. He'd never for a second doubted that any of them wouldn't be there to support him, and time and time again they'd proven him right. The back of his throat tightened, and his eyes stung. So many kids, so many people had been tossed aside for no good reason, and to think of Tripp growing up like one of them hurt his heart more than having to let him go.

Quietly, his mom said, "Why don't you bring him out here? I'll make him see reason."

If only it could be that easy. "I wish." Marty sniffed, wiping his sleeve across his face. "But it doesn't work that way. He has to do it for himself first and foremost. If I made him come out for me, then eventually he'd come to resent me for it."

His mom sighed. "I know you're right. I just wish he'd do right by you."

"Want me to go kick his ass?" Marty jumped when Lily's voice broke into the quiet of the room. "You know I will. In a heartbeat."

Marty laughed. He wouldn't put it past his younger sister, all five feet four inches of her. Everyone in town knew not to mess with Little Lily Fairgrave. The girl could take down ornery steers like the best of them, and he loved her for it.

"No one is kicking anyone's ass. Especially not you, little miss." Buck stepped up behind Lily. "And if anyone really needs it, I'll be the one doing the kicking."

Buck dropped his hands onto Lily's shoulders. He gave her a squeeze and gently moved her so he could step inside, crowding Marty's already too small room.

"Get to the bottom of it, darlin'?"

"What is this?" Marty made eye contact with each of them, but they didn't back down. He was sure he hadn't called a family meeting and really wasn't in the mood for one right now. He just wanted to go to sleep and forget the last couple days. "Some kind of intervention?"

"Marty broke it off with that bull rider because he left him dying in the dirt and didn't give a lick."

"Mom!"

"Well, it's true."

"Then the man does need an ass kicking," Buck said in a tone that sent a shiver down Marty's back. His dad's bad side was extremely rare, and not somewhere anyone wanted to find themselves. Ever.

"Oh my God." Marty huffed out a half-chuckle, half-snort and scrubbed a hand over his face. "No one is kicking anyone's ass. And especially none of you lot. There're plenty of reasons why we're over, and it's not just because of yesterday. It's been coming for a while."

Silence filled the air again. Marty looked down so he wouldn't have to read the expressions on his family's faces, and picked at some lint on his sling. "It was the right thing to do." But there was no heat in his voice to back it up. It was, right? What kind of future could they ever have together if they always had to hide their relationship? Tripp wouldn't even let them be "friends" in public, so what was the point? Tripp had lived that way his whole life, but Marty's whole life had been the exact opposite. Neither knew how to live in the other's world. They just weren't compatible.

Marty started when AC/DC's "Back in Black" rang out from the corner of the room, where he'd tossed his jacket. The ringtone he'd set for Tripp.

The band went into a second repeat of the verse, and Lily turned toward the source. "Are you going to answer that?"

"Nope."

She scowled and grabbed his jacket, searching the pockets until she found his cell phone.

"Lily..."

"It's him." She spoke like she was spitting a bad taste out of her mouth. She raised an eyebrow and held the phone out.

Marty shook his head. "Nothing to say."

His parents shared one of their all-too-familiar silent, speaking glances, and turned back to him.

"It's not working," Marty said. "Breaking it off was the right thing to do. For both of us." Maybe if he said that aloud often enough, he would believe it, but Christ, how could the right thing hurt more than any broken bones ever could?

His dad nodded. "C'mon, ladies." He wrapped an arm around Lily's shoulder and held his hand out for his mom. "Let's all get some shut-eye. Won't do to wake after our guests."

When his mom and sister cleared the room, Buck stepped back inside. He helped Marty up off the bed, snaked a hand behind his neck, and pulled him close enough to press their foreheads together—their "football huddle" of his childhood, when his dad had something important to say to only him. His voice was low and gruff. "Everything will work out as it should, son."

Then Buck was gone, Marty was alone, and the tears came.

Chapter Five

After more than eight weeks of avoiding Tripp's constant phone calls—none of which Marty had listened to because he just couldn't deal with hearing Tripp's voice—there was no avoiding the cowboy back on the circuit. Day two at the Folsom rodeo, and Tripp blasted out of the chute on his third ride of the day—bareback bronco riding.

As always when Tripp rode, Marty couldn't take his eyes off him. No matter how spectacular a bucker the horse he pulled was, Tripp made the ride look effortless. There was no mystery as to why so many up-and-comers idolized Tripp Colby. The man was simply born to it. Pride for Tripp rose in Marty's chest, but the elation quickly spiraled and knifed through still raw wounds that had nothing to do with his run-in with Shockwave. A reminder that he wouldn't be worshipping that finely tuned athletic body ever again.

The whistle blew on what would surely be yet another high 90s scoring ride for Tripp. Bridge and Marty spurred their horses into a gallop and sandwiched the bronco between them. Bridge leaned down and released the flank strap from the bucking horse while Marty kept his horse steady to receive the rider. Tripp threw his arm around Marty's waist and clamped onto his far side hip, then jumped from his money ride onto Marty's horse, Fantom. Marty had no choice but to grab hold of Tripp's shoulder and hold him close until they were clear of the erratic bronc and he could safely let Tripp go.

Marty felt every burning inch of the path Tripp's hands made, even through thick leather gloves, as they slid slowly from his body. Marty pulled Fantom to a stop and let go first, but Tripp held on for a moment longer. Lingering dangerously long for someone terrified to even meet Marty's eyes in public. It was a bold move on Tripp's part, but back on the circuit, seeing Tripp and knowing he couldn't be near him—not that he'd ever been able to beyond their clandestine rendezvous—was proving harder than he'd imagined.

The old Tripp would have been easier to deal with, but the new Tripp, the one making tiny gestures outside his comfort zone, the one who'd decided to add saddle and bareback bronc riding back in to his roster of rodeo talents while Marty had been off reknitting broken bones . . . That Tripp was hard to ignore, hard to keep at a healthy distance. Marty didn't want that chirpy little guy in the back of his mind to start jumping up and down with glee, shouting that Tripp loved him and wanted him enough to finally live out in the open, giving him false hope. Before Tripp, Marty had never seen the inside of a closet. He'd been born out. Still, he couldn't help feeling that Tripp's venture into bronc riding, using the excuse of grabbing onto the pickup man when dismounting a bucking horse, was a first tentative step at cracking that door open.

That excitable little dude named Hope just refused to give up.

But then Tripp's feet hit the ground, and Marty didn't miss the furtive scan Tripp made of the onlookers. It was a look Marty had come to loathe—that stealthy recon to make sure no one saw them together—and Marty had to keep a vital part of himself closed off. He pursed his lips just as Tripp shot him a quick, victorious look over his shoulder—it had been a stellar ride, after all—but the light died in Tripp's eyes at Marty's expression.

No. He would not let that sway him. Tripp had brought this on himself. Marty may have officially ended their relationship, but Tripp was the one who'd been gradually killing it with his refusal to let it see the light of day.

Tripp turned and jogged across the arena, waving at the crowd as he climbed over the rails, while Marty and Bridge hazed the riderless horse out of the arena.

"I saw what that bastard did." Bridge pulled his horse up beside Marty's, and they bumped shoulders. They rode out of the arena together to swap the lighter, faster horses they used for roping and bronco events for the bigger, stockier animals required for the bull riding rounds. Fly was still on the mend and would be for a while yet, so Marty would be riding one of his family's younger geldings, Freaker. In another year, Freaker would rival Fly—if Marty didn't run him into a damn bull.

"Leave it, Bridge."

"He's fucking with you, Smarts. That ain't right."

No, it wasn't, but he wasn't about to get into it again.

Kent stood waiting in the stock area with their fresh horses, and caught the tail end of their conversation. "Who's fucking with whom?"

"No one." Marty dismounted Fantom, handed the reins off, and climbed up on Freaker.

"Three guesses, and the first two don't count," Bridge said.

"What the hell did that asshole do now?"

"I said *leave it*." Marty roughly reined Freaker toward the arena. He'd had enough of that conversation.

He guided Freaker into position in the far corner of the ring and kept his attention focused on the chutes. Seven bulls were loaded and in various stages of prep for their eight-second show, cowboys at the ready double-checking their gloves and ropes and Kevlar vests. Bridge pulled up beside him as the first strains of Queen's "We Will Rock You" blasted from the loudspeakers to signal the rodeo's main event—one that held the same sort of morbid attraction as NASCAR racing. A charged ripple of excitement raced through the crowd. People loved the unpredictability of the bulls, and just like the potential of a big crash on the racetrack, bull riding held the potential for serious injury when one turned on a cowboy.

Scott Gillard was the first cowboy up. Expression intensely focused on the animal beneath him, he tipped his hat to indicate he was ready. Two cowboys pulled the chute open and quickly jumped up onto the rails. A large, red and white bull named Twister lived up to his name, spinning into the arena and launching into a bone-jarring ride.

Tripp would be the final ride to close out the Folsom rodeo, and then Marty could catch a reprieve from seeing him again until the next stop.

Long shadows had begun to chase the sun into dusk by the time the horses had been cooled off, washed down, fed, and settled in for the night. Marty eased into his cheap, fold-up camping chair and lifted his feet up to rest on top of an old, wooden crate.

"Thanks, man," he said when Bridge handed him a beer and pulled up a chair to sit beside him.

"That was a hell of a day." Bridge took a long pull from his bottle. "Glad we've got a few days before we have to be in Salinas."

Marty's chest tightened. Salinas. Where he had first met Tripp.

Tripp had been on a saddle bronc exhibition ride that day and got his hand trapped in the rigging. Bridge had managed to rope the horse and rein him in so they could box the gelding between them long enough for Marty to free Tripp's hand and pull him onto his pickup horse. Tripp had come by after the rodeo, as was customary for the cowboys to stop by and thank the pickup men for keeping them safe. After a handshake that was just a hair longer than was standard for two men, he lingered. They talked for a few minutes about the ride and a couple of the day's highlights, and then the confident, unaffected Tripp Colby suddenly seemed nervous, like he had something more to say but was holding back for some reason. Then he shot a heated look at Marty that set off all kinds of bells and whistles.

Tripp had continued to hang around with a group of cowboys as they regaled their rides and talked strategies, and was the last to leave. He'd started to walk away but looked over his shoulder at Marty, and the parting perusal was clear—he wanted Marty. Tripp cleared his throat, shot a couple of sideways looks, and said good night before disappearing into the darkness of the night.

Aaaand he's in the closet, Marty remembered thinking at the time. That little voice in the back of his mind had told him right then and there that nothing would come of any interest between them. Not when Marty was the "gay pickup man" and Tripp Colby was the star of the professional bull riding world.

But that didn't stop nature from taking its course.

The next day Tripp had shown up at Marty's trailer, late, just as Marty was packing it in for the night. All it took was for Tripp to say "Marty..." in his smoke-roughened voice, and Marty had stepped back, holding the door open for Tripp to enter. No words were spoken again that night. Not until after. And before the faintest sliver of sunlight had snaked across the horizon, Tripp was gone, and the course of their relationship had been set.

The sharp crack of snapping fingers right beside his ear startled Marty out of his thoughts, and beer sloshed over his hand. He cursed, using his jeans as a dry cloth.

"Earth to Smarts." Bridge was wearing an amused smile on his face.

Kent pulled up another ratty chair on Marty's other side, grabbed a longneck from the cooler, and propped his feet up on the crate beside Marty's. He tapped Marty's boots with the toe of his. "Smarts left the planet?"

Marty didn't respond. He took a swig and watched the day's cowboys and roughriders gathering their gear and washing down their horses, some settling in for an overnighter in the backfield of the rodeo grounds, others packing up their rigs and heading straight back out onto the road. Marty zeroed in on a familiar, compact motor coach parked in the farthest corner of the field. Tripp's coach.

Marty tried not to, but his gaze seemed drawn to the vehicle of its own accord. He'd stare without even realizing and consciously have to yank his attention back to his immediate surroundings. To people who wanted to spend time with him, people who weren't afraid of what others thought when they saw them hanging out together.

He watched as Tripp made his way to his home away from home, opened the door, and, as if knowing Marty was watching, turned and glanced over his shoulder. He made eye contact with Marty for all of two seconds. Marty counted. Then turned away and disappeared behind the door.

Several cowboys wandered by to shake his and Bridge's hands and thank them for a job well done. Some stayed for a drink, some just blew through, each blessedly keeping him distracted from thinking about Tripp. Then Kent decided it was high time for a poker game with the few still hanging around and began setting up on the picnic table they'd pulled between their trailers.

"You in, Marty?" He set the chips on the table and looked up.

Marty's "Nope. You guys can keep your money tonight." was met with a hearty round of laughter.

"In your dreams." Bridge got up and walked over to take a seat at the table.

"That much of a card shark, or just saving yourself the embarrassment?"

Marty turned toward the new voice to see Eric standing at the edge of their campsite. He was still dressed in his paramedic gear and cutting a fine impression in the uniform. A soft smile played on his lips, and Marty found himself smiling in return.

"Embarrassment." Bridge had gotten up from the table and was standing next to the crate before Marty even realized he'd moved. "He'd have better luck just leaving his cards face up."

"Shut up," Marty grumbled.

Bridge stepped forward and pulled Eric into a one-armed man-hug. "Nice to see you, Eric."

It might have been Marty's imagination, but did Bridge hug just a bit longer than usual? He watched closely, his gaze shooting back and forth between Bridge and Eric. If he really didn't know better, he'd think Bridge was a little smitten. But no. Bridge was straight. And if he weren't, surely the first people he'd have told would have been him and Kent.

"Good to see you too, man," Eric said.

"Up for a few hands of poker with the guys?"

"Thanks, but no. I'm afraid I'm easy money." Eric smiled, but Marty didn't notice any heat in it. "Maybe next time when you're using popcorn for chips. I just wanted to join Marty for a beer before we roll out."

"Sure. Cool." Bridge shoved his hands into his pockets. "Well, if you change your mind..."

Eric nodded. Bridge shot a sideways glance at Marty and returned to the poker table. Marty frowned. He'd have to ask Bridge what was up with him later.

Eric sat down in the chair Bridge had occupied earlier.

"Ale or lager?"

"Lager, please."

Marty reached into the cooler, grabbed a bottle and shook the excess ice off before handing it to Eric—who couldn't have accidentally brushed his fingers along the back of Marty's hand. Not with the flare of interest in Eric's unwavering gaze. The intention in the gesture was obvious. Marty cleared his throat and leaned back in his chair. Eric popped the cap and held the bottle up, along with a raised eyebrow, and Marty tapped his drink to the neck of Eric's. The glass clinked softly. "Cheers."

Eric settled into his seat and mimicked Marty's posture. "I've heard about you. On the circuit."

"Yeah? What have you heard?"

"That there's no better pickup man in the state of California than Martin Fairgrave. And no gayer one either."

Marty choked on the swig he'd just tipped into his mouth.

Eric laughed and patted Marty's back until he managed to stop choking.

"You good?"

Marty nodded and cleared his throat a couple of times before he felt he could speak, but his voice still sounded croaky. "Didn't know I was that famous, but I suppose I should be happy the first thing my name invokes is my pickup skills."

"Yep, they say you're a roughstock whisperer."

They both broke out laughing. That was one Marty hadn't heard before, but he knew it was what gave him an edge in the arena, why so many cowboys came up to him at the end of the day to express their gratitude, confident they'd get safely out of the ring on his watch.

"So what about you?" Marty swatted at a fly buzzing too close to his drink. "Do you just do local emergency support, or do you follow the circuit? I hadn't seen you before Santa Maria."

"I was just working the local events on my weekends off before, but . . . well, life, you know. Good at throwing curveballs your way when you least expect it. So, I decided to lock up the house for the rodeo season and follow the circuit. Too many of the smaller events have to scramble for ambulance support."

Marty nodded. He'd been at more than one rodeo where events had to be postponed until they had both an ambulance onsite and paramedic support. Even though they were part of the PRCA, some events were so mom and pop he often wondered how they managed to run at all.

"Where is home base then? I'm guessing New York originally."

Eric shifted in his seat and nodded. The tightness in his voice thickened his accent. "Redding. By way of New York."

Judging by the tone and defensive mannerism, Marty knew that was a topic he shouldn't delve into.

"So . . ." Eric turned slightly to face Marty, his head down so that he looked up through his lashes. Long black lashes that framed intriguing violet eyes. "Are you seeing anyone?"

Marty blinked. A low heat infused his cheeks. He looked out over the field. Tripp stood talking with a couple of bull riders from out of state who were loaded up and ready to roll out. As if beckoned, he turned and met Marty's eyes. The back of Marty's throat threatened to tighten, but no, he wouldn't give in to that. He did the right thing, dammit. Tripp Colby was over. The memo was just taking a little longer to work its way through to the big organ in his chest.

He tore his gaze away and took a long draught of his ale to delay speaking until he had enough control to keep his voice steady. "Nope. I'm footloose and fancy-free."

"Is that a good thing?"

Startled by the question, Marty turned sharply to face Eric. "What?"

Eric shrugged. "You went distant there for a second."

Marty regarded Eric for a long moment. Voices, whinnies, and braying danced on the edge of his awareness. "Are you out?"

"Not waving flags, but yes, I'm out."

Marty nodded. "He wasn't. And never will be."

"I'm sorry. Can I be an ass and say I'm hoping his loss is my gain?"

Marty laughed. No way was he about to jump right into anything new just yet. And he'd never been one for casual flings—even though that was pretty much how he and Tripp had started out. But look where that had gotten him. Nope, any gains with Eric would be a long time in coming, if ever. More friends never hurt though, and his instincts told him Eric would make a great friend.

"Maybe we can just stick with the friendship for now?"

Eric nodded, and a kind smile stretched the edges of his mouth. The man was definitely attractive. Marty could even see dating him. Maybe. Someday. He returned the smile.

"So, your friends." Eric tipped his chin in the direction of the picnic-cum-poker table. "Kent and Bridge. Are they single?"

Marty laughed. "They are. Single and straight."

Eric sighed. "Story of my life. The good ones always are."

"Hey, Marty."

His breath caught in the back of his throat when that familiar smoky voice sang like a siren in his heart. He turned to see Tripp standing at the edge of their camping pad, hands in his pockets and a very unusual sheepish expression on his face. Tripp's Adam's apple bobbed a couple of times, and his mouth worked soundlessly before he took a slow breath. "Thanks for keeping me safe out there today."

He nodded, unable to speak just then.

Tripp took a tentative step forward, and a faint sliver of hope drifted into Marty's chest. "Listen, Marty . . . I . . ."

"Got a speech impediment, Tripp?" Marty had been so fixed on Tripp that, once again, he hadn't noticed Bridge get up from the table and move to stand beside his chair. That, or Bridge had developed some sort of stealth superpowers he didn't know about.

Bridge reached down and grabbed a beer from the cooler. "Another cold one, Marty? Eric?" Bridge kept his eyes on Tripp the whole time, and Marty didn't for a second think the exclusion of offering Tripp a drink was unintentional.

Marty shifted his attention back and forth between the two. Bridge looked spring-loaded and ready for action. He twisted his cap off and tossed it into the cooler with one swift flick of his wrist.

Tripp dipped his head enough for the brim of his hat to hide his eyes, then squared his shoulders and lifted his gaze, locking it on Marty. Eric leaned forward in his chair.

"Get yourself lost there, Tripp?" Scott came around the corner with two of his roughrider pals in tow. He stepped up beside Tripp and threw an arm over his shoulder. Tripp froze, and the blank, disinterested, "nothing-gets-to-me" mask he had mastered fell soundly back into place.

"Just saying my obligatory thanks." The thread of sarcasm in his voice cut deep.

"Right." Scott looked over Eric, Marty, and Bridge with an equal measure of disdain for each before giving Marty a curt "Thanks." He steered Tripp around and, making sure his voice carried, said over his shoulder, "Let's go hang out over here with the *real* men."

Marty sighed. The little bit of hope that had ventured out from its hiding place suffered an immediate squashing.

"Pricks." Bridge turned and went back to his poker game.

"What was that all about?" Eric asked quietly.

Marty shook his head and shrugged. "Life, you know."

Chapter Six

Marty slapped cologne on his neck and adjusted his shirt collar in the mirror.

"You're as pretty as you're gonna get, Smarts."

He leaned out of the bathroom and glared at Kent, who was sitting on the small leather couch at the front of his trailer, ankle resting on the opposite knee, and sipping on a beer. "Let's get going before the pool tables are all booked up."

"Yeah." Bridge's voice came from behind the bathroom door.

Marty walked out of the bathroom and laughed. Bridge was standing in front of the long mirror on the backside, fussing with his hair. "I'm the pretty one, am I?"

"Shut up."

Kent tipped his hat back with the mouth of his bottle. "Bridge, you could wear rags and not shower for a month, and the ladies would still be dropping at your feet."

Marty grabbed his boots and crossed the room. "Dropping dead from the stench, more like."

"There is nothing wrong with wanting to look good," Bridge said. "Neanderthals."

Marty shared an amused look with Kent. "Something you want to tell us, Bridge? You're a cowboy. Dirt and sweat is expected. It's a thing, according to the buckle bunnies."

Bridge huffed and, apparently pleased with his appearance, stepped over to the table and snatched Kent's beer out of his hand just as he was about to take a sip.

"Hey!"

Bridge ignored his protest and took an extra-long swig. He had a thing for getting a rise out of people, especially his friends. He belched like a typical cowboy, then reached for his hat. "Dude, you may be fine with the bunnies who like dirt, but I prefer a classier kind of lady."

"Riiight."

"Shut up."

"Both of you ladies shut up." Marty sat on the couch beside Kent to pull on his boots. "You beauty queens ready to go yet or what?"

"Is your friend Eric joining us?" Bridge asked Marty without turning to look at him.

"Yeah, he's meeting us there."

Bridge nodded, and Kent rolled his eyes. Marty glanced between the two of them and frowned. "Did I miss something?"

"Nope." Kent stood up, grabbed his now empty bottle from Bridge, and tossed it in the recycle box under the kitchen counter. "But we approve."

Marty sighed and stood as well. "He's just a friend, guys."

Kent clapped him on the back. "Well, we approve should he become more than a friend."

"*Vamonos o vamos.*" Bridge opened the door, and they headed out into a warm Salinas evening. The sun hung low on the horizon and cast a rich amber glow over the rodeo grounds. The roughstock was all settled for the night, but the soft nicker of horses and occasional bray of cattle drifted on the faint breeze, along with familiar *eau de rodeo*—man and beast sweat, leather, heat and dirt, and the sharp antiseptic odor of topical analgesics and liniment oils for all those aching muscles, both human and equine. Fires flickered about the campgrounds, and the chatter of small groups complemented the song of rodeo roughstock.

Most rodeos held a dance on the last night to wrap up the weekend, and the Salinas site had a large community hall right across the street from the arena, complete with a full bar, live band, and, to Kent's delight, pool tables. If he weren't such a success at roping, Marty had a feeling Kent would be raking it in as a full-time pool shark.

After ensuring the horses were secured for the night and their trailers locked up tight, the threesome marched side by side to the hall. A good-sized crowd had already gathered, and the band was just doing a last-minute sound check before beginning their first set.

Eric popped out of the crowd. "I've got a pool table secured." He pulled Marty into a one-armed hug. He did the same to Bridge, who blushed, and Kent, who squirmed. He was either oblivious to their reactions or chose to ignore them. "What are you guys drinking? First round is on me."

"My kind of man," Bridge said in a low, rough voice. Marty looked over at him. He was smiling at Eric, and as if just realizing how what he'd said sounded, dropped his gaze and cleared his throat. "Yeah. Thanks, man. I'll have a Bud." He walked around Eric and headed toward the pool tables.

Eric looked at Marty expectantly, who in turn looked to Kent, only to be met with the same bewildered expression. Kent shrugged. "I have no idea."

"What?" Eric looked between the two of them.

Marty shook his head. "C'mon, I'll help you with the drinks."

"I have to say." Eric led the way through the crowd to the bar. "If you hadn't known Bridge all your life and confirmed he was straight, I'd have sworn he was gay. Bi at the least."

"Unless he's been holding out on me"—*in which case I'm going to kick his ass*—"he's all about the ladies."

Eric ordered a pitcher of Bud with four glasses and two whiskey shots, then turned to face Marty. He gave a slow perusal from toe to tip before meeting Marty's eyes. "You look good tonight."

Startled by the compliment, warmth spread over Marty's cheeks. He didn't think he was wearing anything all that special: clean jeans free of holes, tears, and stains; a hand-tooled leather belt with a silver Fairgrave Ranch buckle; his snakeskin dress boots; dark blue western shirt—that he just realized Tripp had given him on his birthday—and his black felt cowboy hat with a conch band. He dropped his eyes. "Uh, thanks."

"And you blush adorably."

Marty chuckled and rolled his eyes. "How many shots did you have while waiting for us?"

"Order up!" The bartender pushed two tumblers to the edge of the counter, followed by the rest of their beverages.

Eric paid for the drinks, grabbed the shots, and handed one to Marty. He tapped the rims of their glasses. "Git 'er done, cowboy."

The whiskey burned a scalding path down the back of Marty's throat and up into his sinuses, making his eyes water. He slammed the glass down on the countertop and let out a holler.

"That'll put hair on my chest." He scooped up the beer mugs while Eric laughed and grabbed the pitcher. Marty turned around and slammed into a solid body, just about dropping the glasses. He hadn't realized there'd been anyone behind him, especially hadn't noticed that someone was Tripp.

"Easy there." Tripp's low voice skipped over Marty's eardrums like liquid velvet—or burning whiskey. Tripp gently wrapped his hands around both of Marty's forearms to steady him, though the effect was anything but steadying on his nerves. Marty's eyes locked on Tripp's. Those piercing, ice blue irises as hypnotizing as the very first time he'd looked into them. He gulped. The blood in his veins didn't know whether to flow clockwise or counterclockwise, setting off a rush of jitters in every direction.

"Can we talk?"

What? "Here?"

Tripp looked over Marty's shoulder and glared at Eric. His gaze shifted again, and a flare of panic streaked across his face too fast for most people to identify, unless they'd been staring at the man like there was no one else in the world but him. Like Marty always did, even when he didn't want to.

Tripp jerked his hands back and shoved them into his pockets. He looked toward the bar and cleared his throat. Marty turned to scope the crowd and saw Scott and his cronies settling into a table on the other side of the hall. Scott shot a dark scowl at him before his attention was pulled back to four flashy buckle bunnies. When Marty turned back to Tripp, the man's face was once again expressionless.

When the bartender called order up, Tripp collected a pitcher and strung four beer mugs though his fingers, then covertly leaned into Marty. "I'll find you later."

Marty closed his eyes and took a deep breath. He knew what that meant, and it wasn't going to happen. Not anymore.

"Wow." Eric shook his head, wonderment bright in his eyes. "I'd never have guessed that."

"What?" Marty swallowed hard.

Eric leaned in close so as not to be overheard. "That is one way deep in the closet cowboy." And without waiting for any kind of response or acknowledgment, Eric left a shocked Marty behind and strode off toward the pool tables.

Marty glanced quickly back at the table where Tripp and the homophobe hicks were. One of the girls was leaning in close to Tripp, her hand sliding down his back to tuck into his rear jeans pocket. He turned to her and smiled, then his gaze lifted and caught Marty's. The smile on his face faltered, and Marty turned away. He didn't need to see that. Didn't need the reminder that Tripp would never be able to give him what he needed.

"Let's play some damn pool!" Marty shouted when he arrived at the table and lined up the mugs he'd carried over for filling.

Three hours and too-many-beers-and-whiskey-shots-to-remember later, Kent guided Marty, Bridge, and Eric, who laughed and stumbled like teenage boys, back to their rigs. Kent, who'd never been one for more than a couple of drinks at most, wore the designated walk-the-drunks-home badge.

Bridge tripped over his own feet and just about did a header.

"Children," Kent said halfheartedly, shaking his head.

Marty had his own equine RV, a combo four-horse trailer with living quarters, and Bridge had the same, only his trailer could haul six horses. Kent had one horse to Bridge and Marty's four each, so he traveled with Bridge. Their two rigs were parked perpendicular to each other, so the three were home. Eric didn't travel with horses, but he had a bed set up in the back of his truck.

Kent turned to Eric. "Do you need a designated walker from here?"

"Nope. M'good."

"All right then. See you drunkards at sunup." Kent chuckled, an evil sounding thing, and disappeared inside the trailer he shared with Bridge.

"Yeah, sunup." Bridge hiccupped. He wrapped his arms around Marty, gave him a sloppy kiss on the cheek, then smacked his ass. "Later, Smarts."

"Later, lush."

Bridge turned to Eric and beckoned him closer, then repeated what he'd just done to Marty. Though it seemed to Marty's sideways vision that the kiss on Eric's cheek lasted longer than a peck, and the smack to his ass seemed more like a squeeze. Eric stumbled back when Bridge let him go, his wide-eyed expression no doubt matching Marty's. Then Bridge turned without another word or glance back and staggered to his trailer. After a couple of clumsy tries and colorful curses, he opened the door and tripped up the stairs. A loud thud followed immediately after the door clicked shut. Marty and Eric both laughed.

"Silly bastard probably just passed out right there on the kitchen floor," Marty said.

Their laughter petered out, and an awkward silence filled the air. Eric stared at Marty for a long second, then stepped right up and snaked a hand around the back of Marty's neck, pulling him down into a tentative kiss.

Shocked, Marty couldn't move, didn't know how to respond. The lips on his were soft and seeking but not demanding, willing to wait for him to join in. It couldn't have been more than a heartbeat, though it felt much longer, before the need for human touch overrode the shock of being kissed by someone other than Tripp, and he returned the kiss.

Eric was an attractive man, a good man, and Marty had been enjoying his company. But while the mouth on his gave him a connection he'd been missing, it didn't belong to the right person, didn't move the same way, didn't ignite a firestorm inside his body. Eric pressing against him felt good, but it didn't feel *right*. The frame wasn't as lean, didn't fit the same way to his own.

Eric broke the kiss, his eyes searching Marty's. He slid a hand down, over the front of Marty's jeans. Marty snapped his eyelids shut and groaned not with arousal, but in embarrassment because nothing was awake below the belt.

"Is it me, too much alcohol, or something else?" Eric maintained a slow steady stroke in attempt at getting Marty up.

"It's—" Movement over Eric's shoulder caught Marty's eye, and he froze. At the edge of a spill of light stood Tripp, expression hard, body rigid, fists clenched. Guilt rose like bile in the back of Marty's throat, but a rare burst of anger chased it back down just as quick. He and Tripp were over and done. He didn't owe Tripp anything, had no reason whatsoever to feel bad about moving on, and Tripp sure as hell had no right to the clear display of jealousy.

Eric turned and stepped in front of Marty, which sent a mix of warring emotions through him. On the one hand, he loved that someone would step up and go to battle for him. But on the other hand, he could take care of himself and didn't need anyone to defend him. If it really came down to it, even though he wasn't a fighter, he had a three-inch and twenty-pound advantage over Tripp that he could always leverage in his favor. Though he'd rather use that leverage for more enjoyable activities.

"Is there going to be a problem here?" Eric's accent was heavier and his tone so cold Marty couldn't line it up with the same person.

He placed his hands gently on Eric's shoulders and stepped around him. "It's okay. I'm just going to have a talk with him. I'll see you tomorrow, okay?"

"I don't think so, Marty. Closet or not, I know who he hangs around with, and—"

"It's okay. Trust me."

Whether it was the tone of his voice or the look on his face, he didn't know, but the light changed in Eric's eyes. They widened briefly, and then he nodded. He leaned in and under his breath said, "He doesn't deserve you."

Marty couldn't say anything that would be a denial or an admission. He gave Eric another squeeze. "I'll see you tomorrow."

Eric shot a warning look over his shoulder at Tripp, then, as if for good measure, or simply to taunt the dragon, planted a chaste kiss on Marty's lips. He smirked at Tripp before turning and triumphantly walking away.

Tripp closed his eyes and took a deep breath in an attempt to clear the red smoke from his vision. It hurt more than he could have imagined. Not just seeing Marty in the arms of another, but that Marty seemed able to move on so quickly. How could he just forget about what they'd had so soon?

He waited until the paramedic was out of sight, and took a quick scan of the grounds. All the RVs were dark and quiet; most campfires had burned out completely, though embers still glowed in a few. Livestock was settled, and the only sound was that of coyotes yipping in the distance.

Tripp took another deep breath and carefully approached Marty as if he were a feral horse that would spook at any sudden movements.

"Can we go inside and talk?"

Marty slowly shook his head. "I don't think that's a good idea."

Tripp sighed and scanned the grounds again.

"You're in the shadows, Tripp." Anger laced Marty's usually kind voice and sent a shiver down Tripp's spine. "No one can see you, and no one's around to see you."

Tripp berated himself. He had to stop this, had to get over his fears somehow before he lost Marty completely. The very thing he was trying so hard to break was so ingrained into his being that somewhere along the way it had become instinctive. If he had any chance at all of getting Marty back, he had to find a way out from under the weight of his regrets.

Tripp tipped his chin in the direction the paramedic had gone. "Who was that?"

"A friend."

"Could have fooled me."

"Doesn't matter either way, does it?"

Tripp winced but ignored the jab. He deserved it. "You don't answer your phone anymore or return calls?"

Marty hissed. "God! What do you want from me?"

Tripp surged forward, forcing Marty backward until he hit the side of his trailer.

"Isn't it obvious?" His voice was low enough to be menacing, but just sounded desperate to his ears. "I want *you*."

Marty closed his eyes. Tripp leaned in closer and inhaled deeply. The familiar scents of warm woods and leather and fresh rain acted like a balm to his aching soul and invoked everything he wanted and craved and needed most in this life. God, how he'd missed that smell. Missed Marty. He needed Marty more than he needed to breathe. His fingers twitched to touch, to trace skin and bone and muscle he knew every dip and valley of, to run his hands through the long, dark hair. To simply lie side by side after making love, talking and caressing and just being . . . the only peace Tripp had ever found in his whole fake excuse of a life.

He stretched up so his lips brushed the shell of Marty's ear when he spoke. "Please. Let me in. I need you to let me in."

Marty groaned and opened his eyes. "Don't make this harder than it has to be. Please."

It was the *please* that stabbed Tripp through the heart. He never wanted to hurt Marty, but his demons were just too big for him to control. *Help me.*

"I can't live the way you need to." Marty gently pushed him away. "And you can't live the way I need to."

"I'll come out. I'm trying. I swear."

Half a smile stretched Marty's face, but there was no happiness in it, only a deep melancholy that reflected in his eyes and settled in Tripp's heart. "Do you really want to?"

"I want you back."

Marty shook his head. "That's not what I asked."

"Dammit." Tripp took off his hat and ran a hand through his hair, then fisted it, pulling at the roots until it hurt. That kind of pain he could handle. "What am I supposed to do?"

"Honestly answer that question. Live your life the way you want to. For *you*."

"I can't!" Tripp released his hair and smacked his hat against his thigh.

Marty blinked at the outburst, but his voice was gentle when he spoke. "Why not?"

Tripp looked away and pressed his lips together, hands clenching into tight fists, crushing the brim of his hat as the anger rose in his chest. He wanted to punch something. Break something. Anything. But thank God he at least had enough of a hold on his temper to realize the only immediate things to hit were Marty or the side of the trailer.

Marty didn't deserve it, and the trailer would only do him more damage. Not being able to ride due to a broken hand wasn't worth it. There was only one person who deserved his fist, but he'd made a point of staying far away from that fucker, which right now left him no outlet to release his frustrations.

"Go home, Tripp."

He shook his head but still didn't meet Marty's eyes. He couldn't speak yet, couldn't look at Marty without reaching out, wrapping his arms around him and never letting go. Forget all this soul-searching shit and just lose himself in Marty's touch.

"Go home." Marty rested a hand on his shoulder. "You need to spend some time with yourself."

Tripp closed his eyes at the tender touch, and the back of his throat tightened. "I don't like me."

"Then how is anyone else supposed to?"

Chapter Seven

The better part of a week had passed since Tripp had been told to go home and think about how he really wanted to live his life, and he found himself still looking for the answer at the bottom of a Budweiser bottle. He was deep into his cups when boisterous laughter drew his attention toward the swinging doors of the bar. He spun around on his stool to see Marty, with Bridge and Kent of course, tumble in. The three of them rarely went anywhere solo, but the man following right on their heels was an unwelcome sight. Eric Palmer. The new addition to the little group of musketeers tinted Tripp's vision red, and he ground his teeth. He didn't like how close Eric stood to Marty. Didn't like the way the man looked at him or touched him so often and so freely. The way Tripp should have been doing all along, which would have made Eric a nonissue. But all weekend at the Santa Barbara rodeo, it had seemed as though Eric had been glued to Marty's side, and Tripp couldn't seem to get any closer than a few pickups and the post-rodeo thank-yous.

Laughing. All of them. Even Marty. Like the man had no idea what he was doing to him. But then he had to swallow back the sour taste of his anger yet again. He was the one who had done it to them, after all. That fear of being found out—of what would happen to him, of the guilt over what he'd done to protect himself—had never lessened over the years. Not even after putting as many miles between him and his father as he could the day after he turned of age.

Tripp wanted to try. For Marty, for himself, but memories of the horrible things he'd seen and done all those years ago would rear up in his mind and knock him down again and again. He just couldn't take that final step over the line in sand that had long since hardened to concrete.

His father couldn't touch him now, though. Logically, he knew the man hadn't been able to since the day he'd hightailed it out of town, but it didn't stop the fear that rose to the back of his throat and tried to choke him every time he entertained the idea of doing or saying something in public that would give him away.

Not to mention that his dad's partner at the center they'd called a *retreat*—even though it had been shut down due to public pressure four years prior—was still one of his major sponsors. He'd started rodeoing when he was fourteen years old, first riding steers due to his age, but he'd shown a natural talent for the sport and quickly progressed to the big Brahma bulls. It was a "solid man's sport," his dad had said, and Darren Jackson had stepped up right away as his first sponsor. Even then he hadn't wanted that link to his dad, but he'd known it would be the best way to deflect potential suspicions. Plus, without the help from Jackson Motors, he wouldn't have been able to reach the level of success he'd come to enjoy. Now that he'd won the world championship three years running, he didn't need the funding. He was set for life financially, and the perks that went along with fame were a nice bonus. Then there was the fact he still had two years on his contract, and getting out of it would involve not only lawyers but also the kind of publicity he'd worked hard to avoid all his life. A light chill breezed across the back of his neck, and he shuddered.

Tripp turned to the bartender and ordered a shot of whiskey. Then, like a magnet to metal, his gaze slid back to follow the man he couldn't stop thinking about.

Marty and crew claimed a booth on the far side of the bar but were still well within Tripp's line of sight. He narrowed his eyes when Bridge and Kent took one side, and Eric sidled in beside Marty on the other, which had the two facing him. They sat so close that their shoulders brushed together and set a green fire raging in the pit of Tripp's stomach. He desperately needed to get a grip, or he'd be garnering the kind of attention he'd been avoiding his whole life. The kind that would come from storming over there and breaking Eric's wandering hands.

"Someone piss in your beer?"

Tripp jumped at the sound of Scott's voice and quickly locked his aloof, don't-give-a-shit façade into place. Scott Gillard was the last person he needed to be slipping up around.

"What? No."

Scott pulled up a stool beside him and smacked the palm of his hand on the top of the bar. The bartender turned his way with a raised eyebrow and a glower that went completely ignored. Scott ordered a pint of Bud and a shot of Jack Daniel's, then spun around and cast a considering look at Tripp. It seemed lately that while Eric had been making a point of always being at Marty's side, Scott had been making an equal point of being at his. Every time he turned around, the man was there. Watching with those dark eyes narrowed and a disconcerting expression on an otherwise always-scowling face that Tripp couldn't read but that made him overly self-conscious nonetheless.

Scott sat as still as a snake about to strike. "Something going on?"

A cold sweat crept over skin that felt too tight to contain his secrets. Had he slipped up somehow? Given himself away? Was Scott onto him?

Scott wasn't much bigger than him, roughly about the same height, but he packed more muscle on a solid frame than Tripp did on his lean one. And the cowboy could fight hard and dirty. Whatever it took to guarantee he'd be the last man standing.

Scott leaned forward, scanning the growing crowd, and Tripp willed his pulse to slow while he tracked Scott's line of sight. The regular rodeo weekend party was a big deal in Santa Barbara, where they bypassed the usual community hall dance for the legendary Legless Lizard Saloon. The bar was something right out of the Old West, with rustic wood paneling and floors, high ceiling beams carved from local scrub oak—everything one would expect to see in an old Sergio Leone western. Tripp had always felt a sense of anticipation at the Lizard, like any second he'd see Blondie swagger through the swinging doors, dust-covered poncho hiding a Colt Navy in a worn leather holster, and a cheroot hanging between his sun-chapped lips.

"Christ," Scott bit out. "That fucking sissy and his fag stags are here. Ought to be a fucking law to keep them out."

"He isn't bothering anyone." The words were out before Tripp realized he'd even opened his mouth. *Shit.*

Scott leveled a black glare on him, and if Tripp were questioned on it later he'd swear it was an alcoholic hallucination, but Scott's dark irises flared deep red.

"What the fuck." Scott's voice was low and menacing. He glanced quickly back across the bar. "You taking sides with the girly man over there?"

"Hell no!" Tripp said a bit too quickly, too forcefully, but he held Scott's gaze and issued a warning of his own he hoped read just as clear. "Just wondering why you've got such a hate-on for the man."

The bartender slammed Scott's beer and JD down with more force than necessary. "You'll be minding your business in this here bar, ya hear?" Andrew, according to his nametag, shot a dirty look at Scott. The man was big, definitely spent time in a gym, and his voice was hard as nails. "I run an open establishment for *everyone,* and I aim to keep it that way. We aren't going to have a problem here, are we?"

Scott gave Andrew a disdainful once-over and snorted. "Ain't worth the effort." He slapped a twenty on the counter, claimed his drinks, and downed his whiskey—eyes never leaving the bartender's. He smacked the empty glass upside-down on top of the bill.

"Keep the change, *sweetheart.*" The animosity in his voice was thick enough to halt a stampede dead in its tracks.

He grabbed his beer and spun around on his stool to face the crowd. Tripp cast a quick apologetic look at Andrew, who just shook his head and walked away.

"Fucking bleeding heart liberals," Scott said to no one in particular, and took a swing of his beer.

Making a point not to look across the bar again, Tripp turned his back to Marty's table. But that didn't stop the awareness of the man behind him or the overpowering urge to spin around and look.

"Now that's what I'm talking about," Scott drawled in a lewd voice.

Tripp followed his line of sight to see three flashy-looking women entering the saloon. He took a deep draught of his Budweiser to prevent a groan on the edge of escape and geared himself up to act the old, hot-for-chicks-straight-guy role. God, he was growing weary of this charade. Always having to watch what he said, who he talked to, how he looked and acted.

You know how to end it. The demon horse in his mind reared up, striking the inside of his skull with its sharp hooves, and a shudder ran through him.

Someone needed to shoot that beast once and for all. Right between the fucking eyes.

Tripp chugged back the last of his beer and signaled to Andrew for another, as well as another shooter. He'd need it for the long night this was shaping up to be.

"Actually." He stopped before Andrew turned away. "Make that two shots. Four fingers."

Marty tried to keep his focus on the conversation at hand, but his thoughts kept wandering back to Tripp sitting across the bar. He hadn't seen Tripp when they'd first arrived, but from his seat facing the bar, he couldn't miss the man.

He frowned when he noticed the bartender lining up two shots in front of Tripp. He didn't know how long Tripp had been there, but from the looks of things, he seemed well on his way to a nasty hangover.

It seemed that Eric had noticed too. He was a tactile person in general, but tonight Marty got the feeling it was more for show—a subtle poke at Tripp—than anything else. Marty couldn't deny he liked the feel of the hand resting against his thigh. He liked the brush of a solid shoulder against his, the bump of a knee. He glanced at Eric, animatedly describing an episode on the job with a belligerent drunk who'd refused to go to the hospital, even though he'd had a long roofing nail sticking out of the side of his head. Eric Palmer was an attractive man. There was no denying it. And he seemed comfortable with who he was. He didn't care what other people thought and didn't hesitate to express how he felt through actions both subtle and grand.

If only Tripp could be like that. If only he weren't so afraid. Marty wasn't sure exactly what it was in Tripp's past that had such a death grip on him, but whatever it was scared the pants off a cowboy who stared down two-thousand-pound bulls for a living. Somehow, someday, the man had to find his way out from under that shroud of fear, if for no other reason than his own health and well-being. A dark ache crept into Marty's chest at seeing how much of a toll Tripp's secrets were taking on him.

If only Tripp would trust in himself enough to let it all go. Trust in Marty.

Marty let himself imagine for a moment that the man sitting so close to him was Tripp and not Eric. He didn't think that was too much to ask for. Someone not afraid to sit with him, for people to know they were friends and even more, to show how they felt for each other beyond closed doors.

Eric had come to the end of his tale, not that Marty heard enough to get anything more than the gist of it, and his three friends howled, tears streaming down their cheeks. Marty smiled and his attention slid back to the bar. Rather, the cowboy at the bar in the snug-fitting Wranglers that highlighted all the right attributes, and the dark blue shirt with the sleeves rolled up to the elbows to reveal tanned, muscular forearms.

Not as covertly as he probably thought he was being, Tripp shifted on his stool and ventured a glance Marty's way. Their gazes clashed and locked, and a shot of heat raced up Marty's spine before dive-bombing back down to pool in his groin. He spread his legs a little wider, and his knee pressed against Eric's, which Eric misread as a sign to engage.

Eric draped his arm over Marty's shoulders and leaned in. Moist heat and soft lips brushed the shell of his ear as Eric whispered in a low, rough voice, "I want to take you back to my trailer and ride you like a wild mustang hell-bent on bucking me off."

The words bounced around the inside of Marty's head while his eyes remained steady on Tripp's, tangling up with his growing arousal and sending confusing signals to his brain. God, how he wanted Tripp right then. Wanted to stand up, close the space between them, pull Tripp to him until their bodies were pressed as tightly together as possible, and take that mouth with his. Savor and worship and devour.

Marty felt the groan slip from his lips without hearing it, but he knew someone had heard. The warmth of a hand landed on his thigh and moved upward, closing in on his growing erection. Just one touch would be too much.

Tripp's expression darkened. His lips pressed tighter together, and his body tensed. Marty's desire shifted into annoyance. Tripp had no right to be angry, had no right to ask or demand anything of Marty, who'd made every concession to appease Tripp where Tripp had done nothing in return. Their entire relationship had been solely on Tripp's terms from day one, and Marty wasn't having any of that anymore.

Forgetting how close Eric had moved in during his moment of fury, Marty turned, and their noses bumped. Before he realized it, Eric's mouth was on his. The kiss stunned him still for a second that seemed so much longer. Misfiring synapses reset with a jolt when he felt the requesting nudge of a hot wet tongue on the seam of his lips, and he jerked back.

Silence settled over their table, music from the jukebox faded, voices drifted away on an unfelt breeze, and the only sound that registered in his mind was the deafening, unmistakable report of shattering glass. He turned toward the sound to see Tripp standing up, holding half a broken beer bottle in his hand. Amber liquid streaked with thin trails of red slid over his skin and dripped to the floor.

Tripp looked directly at Marty and shot him a killing glare before turning on his boot heels and storming out of the saloon. Sound screamed back so fast Marty felt the need to hang on to something bolted down or be blown over by the force of it.

He glanced around the table. Kent wore an expression of surprise and amusement, Bridge didn't seem any happier than he was, and Eric still had heat in his eyes, but Marty could swear there was a spark of mischief in their violet depths.

"What the hell was that all about?"

"What was what?" Marty couldn't tell if the confusion was legit or if Eric was just that good an actor.

"Draaa-maaa..." Kent singsonged under his breath.

Marty leveled a warning glare at Kent, who raised his hands in surrender, then lowered them to reach for the oversized plate of nachos they'd all been sharing, quieting himself with an exaggerated bite.

Marty glanced at Bridge again, who still hadn't said a word, and was now staring off into the distance and chewing on his bottom lip. He only did that when something was bugging him. Marty needed to find out what was going on with him lately, but right now there was Eric.

He turned to face the man in question. "That was over the line."

"I didn't realize we had a line."

Okay, Marty had to give him that. They hadn't actually had a chance to talk much since the kiss the week before. Not only was the Santa Barbara rodeo one of the bigger events on the circuit, keeping Marty and Bridge on the go the whole time, but Eric had been called away early the first day to cover shifts for another paramedic. The time they did manage to spend together had been as a group.

"I'm not looking for more than a friend right now." Marty lowered his voice. A bar full of cowboys wasn't the most conducive place for that particular discussion, but he needed to set things straight before more than what was available was expected. "I can't deal with more than that."

A flash of disappointment doused the heat in Eric's eyes, and he looked away, pulling his hand from Marty's thigh and removing his arm from around Marty's shoulders. He shifted slightly to open up space between them.

"I get it," he said.

Marty sighed. "I enjoy your company. I do. I truly want us to be friends, but I can't give you more. Think we can do that?"

Eric nodded, then looked up and met Marty's eyes with a not-quite-genuine smile. "Yeah, sure. We can do that."

"Thank God that's all settled." Kent swiveled in his seat and flagged down a waitress. "Round of tequila shots for my boys here, darlin'! We got some toasting to do."

"No, make it . . ." She was gone before Marty could finish. ". . . three."

Kent raised his eyebrows. "What? You can't wimp out on us, Smarts."

"Not wimping, dude." Marty stood and grabbed his hat from a hook on the side of their booth. "It was a crazy weekend, and I'm exhausted, so I'm going to call 'er done."

Kent frowned. Eric watched him closely, like a dog waiting for the magic word that meant walk time, and Bridge still seemed lost in thought.

Grateful they'd come in two trucks, he turned to Eric. "You mind giving them a ride back?"

Expectation faded from Eric's eyes, and he nodded, smile firmly in place. "No problem. I'll make sure they make it back in one piece."

"Thanks. See ya, guys."

Less than fifteen minutes later, Marty pulled into the slumbering rodeo grounds, and when his headlights splashed across his trailer, they lit a form in the shadows. He sighed. He didn't have to see more than that quick flash to know who was lurking there in the dark.

He killed the engine and sat for a moment, watching the spot where he'd seen Tripp. Nothing moved. No sound reached his ears but the tick of the cooling motor and the serenade of crickets. Finally he stepped down from his truck, and the shape detached from the shadows until Tripp stood before him, hands in his pockets, posture tense and rigid.

His voice was barely audible. "Marty. Please . . ."

Chapter Eight

The pained sound of Tripp's voice ripped at Marty and spurred him into action. He stepped past Tripp to unlock the trailer and flick the lights on, then held the door open for Tripp to precede him inside. Tripp didn't meet his eyes as he climbed the two steps into Marty's home on the road. Marty followed him in and quietly closed the door. He took off his cowboy hat and tossed it onto a chair nearest the entrance, but he didn't move any farther inside. Tripp stood in the middle of the small living room with his back to Marty, shoulders slumping as tension slipped from his muscles, head tipped down slightly.

When Tripp remained motionless, Marty sighed.

"Sit down."

Tripp didn't move, so Marty waited. Aside from a rustic table clock set in a horseshoe that sat on a shelf, steadily ticking off the seconds, there was only the silence of the sleeping world around them. The unfaltering beat of the clock combined with the waning alcoholic buzz to lull his tired body to the point where he startled at Tripp's smoky voice.

"I want to come out. I do. But I . . . I can't." Tripp's voice was low and small, the words stilted, like newborn colts testing out their wobbly, too-long legs for the first time. "He . . . he found the magazine. Took me to that . . . *place*."

Tripp's entire body shuddered, and Marty fought the urge to go to him.

"I was just a kid. So fucking scared." Tripp snapped off the last word hard. He clenched his hands into fists so tight his knuckles turned white. "And I-I . . . *Fuck*."

The pain in Tripp's voice echoed in Marty's chest. Even if he couldn't be with him the way Tripp needed, he'd never loved anyone like he loved him and couldn't bear to see him hurting so badly.

"What happened?"

Tripp shook his head vehemently. He raised trembling fists as if preparing to punch something, but the shaking increased, and he dropped them limply to his sides. Marty took a step forward, but froze when a tremor wracked Tripp's entire frame and a rare, strangled sob escaped his mouth. That beautiful head tipped down, and the defeated posture tugged hard on Marty's heart. He wanted to pull Tripp into his arms and hold him tight. He'd never seen Tripp so torn up and wasn't sure if he needed comfort or space, so he placed a hand lightly on Tripp's shoulder. The muscles beneath his palm bunched, then Tripp's whole body went slack. He spun and threw his arms around Marty, holding on so fiercely Marty felt like his lungs had been locked into a vise grip. Tripp's hat fell to the floor as he buried his face into the crook of Marty's neck, and another of those strange, heartbreaking sobs escaped from one of the strongest men Marty had ever known.

The pain radiating from Tripp was more than Marty could bear. He returned the embrace just as tightly, letting the man he'd love until his dying day know he wouldn't let go. He'd be there for him and help him get through whatever past traumas tormented him.

"I . . . Timothy . . ." The moist breath of Tripp's muffled voice warmed a patch on Marty's chest, dampening his shirt. "Fuck. Timothy."

A million questions ran through Marty's mind, but he knew this was not the time. The man in his arms didn't need questions right now; he just needed a little human comfort. "Shhh, I've got you now. It's going to be okay."

Tripp gripped Marty harder, pulling at his shirt. "No. They won't let me go."

Marty moved one hand up to cup the back of Tripp's head and slid his fingers through soft hair. "They will"—*whoever they are*—"if you make them."

"I want to be what you need. I want to be that man who's . . . not afraid to stand tall and proud at your side. But he's . . . he's not me."

"Yes." Marty rubbed his head against Tripp's, then placed a soft kiss on his temple. "Yes. He can be."

"No." Tripp's voice was quiet, resigned, and his grip loosened. "I've done terrible things. Unforgivable things."

"I don't think anything can be that bad," Marty said. Tripp remained silent, motionless except for his settling but still erratic breathing. "Everything can be forgiven, if the remorse is genuine and restitution is made."

Silence closed in around them, and the awareness of Tripp tensing up again hit Marty before the man released his hold and pulled away. Tripp kept his head down, turning around quickly, and Marty felt a cold chill take him over, not only from the loss of Tripp's body pressed to his, but also from the physical chasm now between them.

Tripp's voice was hard when he spoke. "Not everything. You can't ever make up for destroying someone else's life."

"You don't have it in you to ruin a life. Not deliberately. You're not that kind of person."

Tripp glanced over his shoulder, eyebrows raised. "But you can push people too far and know that you are as you're doing it. What does that make you then, if you keep pushing until that person reaches their breaking point?"

Marty didn't quite know how to respond to that, but he knew Tripp well enough to know there had to have been extenuating circumstances that drove him to it, if he had truly done something like that. Self-preservation could be a powerful motivator.

"Did you push someone that far?"

"Maybe. Yes." Tripp let out a frustrated huff and ran a hand through his hair. "Hell, I don't know. But I put the wheels in motion."

Marty leaned to the side a little to watch Tripp in profile. "Can you tell me what happened?"

Tripp looked around the room until his gaze landed on the 1892 lever-action cowboy rifle encased in a glass box on the wall above the leather couch. His attention fixed on the rifle, he spoke in choppy sentences, his voice devoid of emotion.

"My dad found a magazine. *Playgirl*. Stuffed between my mattress and box spring. He blew a gasket. Went on and on about how homosexuality was the work of the devil. No son of his would be such a sick deviant. He'd rather me dead." He paused to let out a hollow huff-chuckle. "Oh, but he had a cure."

A cold chill ran through Marty as the meaning of those last words took form. More questions shot forward, but he waited for Tripp to continue on his own. He knew Tripp was sharing something he'd never before put voice to, and how hard it had to be for a man who kept so much of himself hidden from the world.

Tripp dragged his hands down his face and dropped his gaze to the couch. "They sent him there. To the center. And it destroyed him. *I* destroyed him."

"Wait. You lost me. Who sent who where?"

Tripp continued as though he hadn't heard anything.

"He wasn't out, but I knew he was gay. His parents were good friends with mine. I had to deflect. I knew what would happen if my dad found out about me, and I was terrified. So I... I outed Timothy. Now do you see? It was because of me he was sent there, and everything that happened after was my fault."

"No. It wasn't. You were just a kid, right?" But Tripp didn't acknowledge his question. "You couldn't have known what would happen. No one could have. You were young and frightened and acted out of fear. Most kids would."

Tripp spun around to face Marty and pinned him with intense, red-rimmed eyes, his expression imploring. "I *knew* what went on at the center. My dad *owned* it." He pursed his lips. "When my dad found that magazine... God. He was livid. He dragged me outside and threw me in the car. I didn't even have socks on. It was winter, snowing, and I had no jacket. He took me there. Took me inside and showed me what they did to men like me. How they *corrected* them. Holy Christ, Marty. The things I saw . . . I couldn't let anyone know about me. Not ever."

The fire drained from Tripp's eyes. He lowered his head and seemed to sink in on himself—his whole stance was that of a broken man, and he looked small . . . so small. The reedy rasp of his voice nearly broke Marty's heart. "So I ratted out a sweet, happy kid and ruined his life to save mine."

There, Tripp thought, keeping his gaze locked on the sharp, colorful angles of the southwestern throw rug under his feet. *The demon horse is out. Finally*.

But instead of relief, all he felt was exhaustion. He'd rather have bamboo slivers driven under his fingernails than ever go through that again.

Silence descended like an oppressive mass in his chest while he waited for what would surely come next: Marty's steel-tipped boot to his ass as he kicked Tripp out the door and out of his life forever. But at least now Marty knew. Coming out now, living truly free and happy would be like stomping on the bones of the suffering Timothy had no doubt endured. That dark cloud would forever overshadow his life.

Marty took two long strides forward, and Tripp braced himself, imagining this time it would be his once-gentle giant grabbing him by the scruff of the neck and tossing him out. Instead, Marty engulfed him in a strong embrace, arms like steel bands holding him tight to the solid, warm body that he had missed more than he could ever express.

He wrapped his arms around Marty and clawed at the back of Marty's shirt, fisting the soft material in his hands while his body began to shake uncontrollably. He should have known Marty would never react like his father. He let himself melt into the sanctuary that was Martin Fairgrave, clutched at him tighter, remembered how good it always felt to let his barriers down and simply *be* with this man.

With their heads pressed together, Marty's breath gusted across Tripp's ear. "I can't begin to imagine the toll it's taken on you to carry that for so long, but I understand now. Your father can't touch you anymore, Tripp. No one can. Deep down, you know that, right?"

Tripp nodded because that's what Marty needed from him, but he didn't want to talk anymore, didn't want think about anything. All he wanted was to lose himself in the touch and heat and skin of the man who was holding him so reverently.

"Marty. Please." His voice came out in a broken whisper. "Make it stop. Make me forget. Please."

Marty shushed him, keeping his embrace strong and coaxing him into an easy sway. "I'm here. I've got you."

Marty continued to whisper assurances in his ear. The mollifying tones of his voice, the rhythmic rock of their bodies, and the steady *tick-tock* of the clock worked in unison to create a soothing lullaby. The last strains of tension leeched from Tripp, and he relaxed further. The tremor that had been running steady since the saloon faded; the dark memories that had ridden in on the back of the demon horse retreated.

Tripp loosened his grip around Marty's waist a fraction, enough to unclench his hands from Marty's shirt, but there was no way he was going to let go of this man anytime soon. He may never have true happiness, but as long as he had Marty, he'd have the next closest thing.

With his palms flat, he began a slow caress of Marty's muscular back, one hand moving progressively higher while the other moved lower. By the time his right had tangled into Marty's hair, his left had settled into the small of Marty's back, fingertips dipping just below the waistline of his jeans.

He pressed his growing erection against Marty, relieved to be met with an answering hardness.

Marty groaned deep in his throat. "Tripp—"

"Please," he whispered as he pulled Marty's head down, angling his own upward. He *ached* to feel Marty, to taste him, and his need increased to near panic level. "I *need* to forget."

He brushed his lips tentatively against Marty's in quiet question, testing, teasing, begging, and when Marty responded by gently sucking on Tripp's lower lip, a shiver skittered across the surface of his skin. A wake of heady tingles sent a burst of bright energy charging into his depths. That was what he needed. No thinking, just sensation, Marty.

Tripp slanted his head to deepen the kiss, opening his mouth to welcome Marty's tongue and flavor inside. He sucked and savored and reveled, and his heart pounded in his chest like an Indian war drum. He broke the kiss long enough to whisper against Marty's lips, "God, I've missed the taste of you."

Before Marty had a chance to respond, Tripp reclaimed his mouth, but this time he couldn't control his need. Fervor took the reins, and he brought both hands up to cup Marty's head, kissing deeper, insistently, until tongues dueled and teeth bumped and his mouth flooded with sweet moisture. Sure fingers twined in his hair, tugging his head back. *Yes. This. More.* But he couldn't get the words out, couldn't break the connection, so he moaned what he meant, and Marty understood, God bless him.

Marty dropped one hand to Tripp's ass and lifted, forcing their groins hard together. The pressure against his constricted cock was painfully exquisite, the solid feel of Marty's dick so close, so ready, glorious. But it wasn't enough. There were too many layers between them. Too much keeping him from the only thing that mattered most in this world.

Tripp pushed with his whole body until Marty accepted the unspoken demand and let him guide them into the bedroom. When the backs of Marty's knees hit the edge of the bed, Marty gripped him tighter and pulled Tripp down with him. They crashed onto the plush mattress. Their impassioned kiss finally broke as the impact forced a whoosh of air from their lungs.

Time paused for just a second while he indulged in the man underneath him: dark hair in disarray, eyes glinting with desire, shirt partly pulled up to reveal a hint of pale skin—skin Tripp needed to see more of. He attacked the buttons like a charging bull, mumbling as he went, "This damn shirt has to go."

A soft chuckle drew Tripp's attention and his mission stalled under the force of a smile so genuinely sweet that it reached deep inside of him, softened the rough edges and chased away the shadows.

Good God, I love you.

He frowned. Still he couldn't voice the words he needed to say most.

Marty reached up and caressed his cheek with callused fingertips, then slid his hand around the back of Tripp's neck.

"Come here," he rasped.

Tripp obliged.

Marty's lips were hot and silky moist, and the feel and taste of him sent a rush of charged adrenaline coursing through Tripp's veins.

Marty pulled back and licked his lips while keeping his gaze locked on Tripp's mouth. "Show me what you need."

That was a request Tripp could never deny his gentle cowboy. He peppered kisses over Marty's nose, his eyebrows, mouthed his jawline, and nipped down the column of his neck. He sucked on the corded muscle there, reveled in the salty taste of warm skin. Skin he'd so desperately missed exploring.

Marty hissed and slid his hands under Tripp's shirt, and every touch felt like a brand that he welcomed wholeheartedly. To be marked forever as belonging to Marty Fairgrave . . . he couldn't imagine anything better.

Tripp pushed Marty's shirt open and urged him to sit up so he could slide it over broad shoulders, down defined arms, and off. Marty claimed his mouth again in a demanding, intense kiss, then pulling Tripp with him, reclined back to the bed. Marty rocked his hips, grinding their groins together, and Tripp fought the release his body begged for. That would come, holy hell, that would come, but not until he worshipped every inch of the body beneath him. He lifted slightly and shoved a hand between them, making quick work of opening both of their jeans to free their straining cocks.

Tripp sat up, and Marty chased him with his mouth, letting out a small cry of remorse when Tripp broke off the kiss so he could shimmy down the bed.

He tugged at the waistband of Marty's jeans, his voice rough and scratchy with need. "These have to go."

Marty nodded and lifted his hips so Tripp could rid him of the offending clothing. Tripp stood and finished stripping himself, then froze at the sight of Marty stretched out before him, lazily stroking the most beautiful penis Tripp had ever had the pleasure of enjoying. He lifted his gaze to meet Marty's, and another rush of charged heat cascaded through his veins.

He crawled back onto the bed and began kissing and nipping a crooked upward path along Marty's strong legs. Tripp spoke the only way he knew how when the words refused to come: with his body. He poured all the love and desire and reverence he felt for his gorgeous cowboy into their lovemaking. He made his words clear with every touch, caress, and kiss.

Marty jolted and a hiss escaped his mouth when Tripp sucked at a patch of skin on his inner thigh.

"Like that, do you?"

"You know it."

"Me too." Tripp wrapped one hand around the base of Marty's cock and cupped his balls with the other. "But I like this more."

He licked his lips, then dropped his head and swallowed Marty down as deep as he could take him. Marty jerked up and a jumble of vowels and half-words spilled from his throat. Tripp celebrated the bittersweet taste of silky, hard flesh in his mouth, the hands tangled in his hair, holding but not directing or forcing. He sucked and swirled his tongue around the hot shaft, up and down in a counter rhythm with his hand. Again and again, making sure Marty understood what he was saying with his mouth, his tongue, his hands.

Marty tugged at his hair, but he was too enraptured to pay attention until the pull became hard enough to hurt.

"Stop," Marty ground out. "Don't want to come yet."

Tripp slid off slowly, sucking as he went. The sight of Marty's eyes rolling to the back of his head sent a rush of pride through him, knowing he was the one driving Marty to the edge of ecstasy. He smiled when Marty's focus settled on him again, a teasing grin stretching his mouth. Tripp reached up and traced the plush lower lip with his fingertip. That was one of the many things he loved about Marty; he was so easy to make happy.

Tripp gave Marty's cock a slow, caressing stroke and then reached over to the night table to retrieve a bottle of lube Marty always kept there for his midnight visits. Holding Marty's gaze, he poured a dollop into his palm, then cupped his hands together and blew heat into the cavern they created. Satisfied the liquid was warm enough, he ran both slippery hands over Marty's length. He straddled Marty's hips and lined himself up.

Just as the tip of the cockhead touched Tripp's hole, Marty tensed, and a flash of panic lanced his expression.

Tripp stopped, immediately understanding. "Unless you have a reason to, we still don't need condoms." Five months into their secret relationship, and after clean test results, they had stopped using them. Tripp may have forced their relationship to stay in the closet, but he had been and still was faithful.

"I'm sorry."

Tripp didn't like the thread of regret in Marty's voice. "Nothing to be sorry for, babe." And there wasn't. Marty knew he'd been a bit of a dog before they'd met, discreetly hooking up when and where he could, so he couldn't fault the man. Tripp bent down and kissed Marty, languid and deliberate, and then slowly seated himself on Marty's shaft. The familiar burn of being stretched and filled sent shivers of delight cascading over his skin. Marty's hands ran a hot path from his thighs to hips, their tongues continued their sensual duel, and the world righted itself.

Marty broke the kiss, and in a deep, ragged voice said, "Ride me, cowboy."

Tripp tapped his forefinger to an imaginary hat, then mimicked tossing it aside. "Happy to oblige, buckaroo."

Marty's laugh died on a drawn out moan when Tripp began to rock his hips, and they quickly settled into a practiced rhythm. Grunts and groans and harsh breaths rose and fell, creating discordant yet somehow beautiful music. The rich chorus seeped into Tripp's chest, and its echo set the dark hollows of his mind alight with each well-played note.

"Tripp..." Marty panted, and Tripp knew his cowboy was close. He was too, but he wanted Marty to come first, wanted to feel the heat coat his insides.

"Go," he said.

And Marty did. The thick veins in his neck stood out in stark relief, his body tensed, a dark blush spread across his chest, and he bucked up hard into Tripp. Good God, if that wasn't the most erotic thing Tripp had ever seen. And the last thing he saw before his eyes clamped shut and pinpricks of white flashed behind his lids. He came with such intensity he could have sworn the whole trailer shook. All without a single touch to his dick.

When the convulsions of blissful orgasm receded, he slowly lifted off Marty, who groaned and reached out to pull Tripp to him. Tripp went willingly, pillowing his head on Marty's shoulder. Marty tucked him into his side and pressed a soft kiss to his temple.

"We should clean up," Tripp said after their breathing returned to normal and he could think clearly again. "Turn the lights off."

Marty nodded but didn't make any effort to follow through. Just when Tripp thought he'd fallen asleep, he mumbled "later" in a heavy, sated voice.

Yeah, later.

"Missed you," Tripp whispered when Marty's breathing deepened and leveled out. Just before he drifted off, he added, "Love you."

Chapter Nine

Tripp parted the window blind slats with a finger and peered out into the predawn rodeo grounds. More than half of the weekend's competitors and the roughstock supplier had already pulled out the night before and headed for their next stop on the circuit. Only those who'd delayed the road a day to kick up their boots at the Legless Lizard remained, and a good number of those were probably sleeping it off in the beds of local buckle bunnies.

Hopefully luck would be on his side, and one of those waking up elsewhere would be Scott. The man was serious about his bunnies—even had a regular on the northern stops of the circuit.

Tripp let the slat fall back into place, then turned to finish buttoning up his jeans and froze.

Marty was half sitting up in bed, resting on one elbow, his hair sleep-styled into a sexy mess that begged for Tripp's fingers, and the bedsheet pooled around his waist to obscure what Tripp knew would be an impressive morning wood. Maybe he could postpone his departure a little bit longer.

"Are you leaving?"

The restrained, almost accusatory tone in Marty's voice drew Tripp's focus from the body to the man. That was when he noticed the blank expression, the way Marty's usually warm, open eyes seemed flat as if in effort to conceal his thoughts, and his lips set in too straight a line.

Tripp cleared his throat as guilt rose cold and constricting in his chest. "I . . . uh."

He looked away and spotted his shirt on the floor at the foot of the bed. He needed to get dressed and get to his RV before anyone was up to notice him leaving. He needed to take his jeans off and get back into bed with Marty, lose himself in that peaceful haven. He didn't want to keep hiding, but he didn't know any other way to be. Even after telling Marty the truth, he still heard the distant thunder of hooves in the back of his mind when he let himself start thinking that things could be different.

The war between his desires and fears held him firmly in place, unable to move in any direction, unable to vocalize the chaos that plagued him.

"You need to deal with this." Marty's was voice softer now, the tone laced with an edge of concern.

Hooves pounded harder, grew louder. Tripp bent down and snatched up his rumpled shirt. He shook it out with jerky movements and shoved his arms into the shirtsleeves. "I can't right now."

"Then when?" Marty tracked his movements but didn't meet his eyes. "They won't go away on their own."

"You think I don't know that?" Tripp's voice rose a notch. "You don't know what it's like to have a father who would rather kill you than accept that you're gay, or how fucking terrifying coming out can be. You've always been out, always been accepted."

Marty's head tipped back slightly, eyebrows lifting just enough for Tripp to feel less than two inches tall. *Fuck.*

Marty sat up straight. He dropped his gaze and smoothed the sheet over his lap. Then he looked up and opened his mouth to speak, but frowned when the muffled galloping beat of the *Bonanza* theme song filled the air between them. Marty had a different ringtone for everyone—"Back in Black" for Tripp, the *James Bond* theme for Kent, "Misirlou" for Bridge, and "Bonanza" for his family. Even though Tripp was grateful for the timing, it seemed unusually early for a family call.

Marty ignored the phone until the room fell silent again. "True, I've always been out, and I can't live any other way. But don't think I've had a smooth ride my whole life. I *do* know what it's like to be bullied. I *do* know what it's like to fear for my life in certain situations simply because I'm gay." Marty paused when

"Bonanza" started up again, but spoke over it. "And it doesn't take a degree in rocket science to know your fears won't go away until you—"

"Are you going to get that?"

Marty narrowed his eyes. The phone stopped. "If you keep hiding, then they win. Fear isn't bigger than you, Tripp. What you do for a living has the potential to kill you every single time that chute opens. Not this. You have to take its power away."

Tripp clenched his jaw. He so did not want to have this conversation right now. Maybe never. His feet itched to turn and run, heels already lifting off the ground, while the muscles in his arms coiled like springs. Run, fight, go, stay, all it did was hurt his head and keep him frozen in no-man's-land. And the fucking "Bonanza" started up again.

"Answer the goddamned phone."

Marty glared daggers at him, then ripped the sheet off his body and jumped from the bed. Tripp remained frozen, gaze tracking the movements of a gloriously naked Marty rooting through the pile of clothes on the floor. He dug his phone out of a jeans pocket and flipped it open just before the last refrain ended. "What?" His voice and expression were immediately contrite. "No. I'm sorry, Ma. I'm up. Just dealing with a"—he glanced at Tripp—"situation. What's going on?"

All color drained from Marty's complexion, his mouth fell open, and he nearly missed the bed when he collapsed on the edge of it. "Oh God."

A chill brushed across Tripp's skin.

Marty's voice was nearly inaudible. "What happened?"

Tripp could hear a woman's voice on the other end, but couldn't make out the words, only the frantic tone.

"How is he?" Marty jumped up, tucked the phone between his ear and shoulder, and began dressing. He nodded, and then said in a stronger voice, "Thank God. Are they keeping him overnight?" He hiked his jeans up but left them open while he pulled on his shirt. "Okay. I'm leaving now, but I'm about seven hours away. I'll meet you at the ranch." He made quick work of his shirt buttons. "I will. Love you too."

He ended the call and tossed the phone onto the bed, tucked his shirttails into his jeans, and did up the fly and belt. Sitting down to pull on his boots, he seemed oblivious of Tripp still standing there and of their unfinished discussion.

"What happened?"

"My dad." Marty stood and scanned the room. He snatched up his phone and stuffed it into his jeans pocket. Then he grabbed Tripp's boots and shoved them at him as he left the bedroom. "He's been in an accident. I have to go home."

"Christ. I'm sorry. Is he going to be okay?" Tripp stepped into his boots and followed Marty into the living room.

"Sounds like. Mom's going to need help with the ranch while he's out of commission though." Marty grabbed his hat off the chair by the door and turned to him. He rocked on his feet and slid his hands along the brim of his hat. Tripp understood. Family took precedence.

"Go." Tripp bent down to retrieve his hat from the floor where it had fallen the night before.

"Last night doesn't change things between us. I told you I'd be there for you, and I will be. But not as your secret boyfriend."

Tripp was in no rush to deal, but he acquiesced with a nod anyway. "See to your dad."

They stepped outside into a cool Southern California morning. The faintest brush of sunrise streaked a thin line across the eastern horizon. Before they parted ways, Marty turned an imploring look on him. "See to yourself. Please."

Chapter Ten

Marty watched swirls of dust chase a familiar midnight blue Ford F-150 making its way up the long drive to the main house, and a rush of excitement urged him to his feet.

"Who've we got here?" Buck said from his perch on the front porch, where they'd been sitting while Marty took an afternoon break from ranch chores to share an iced tea with his dad.

Even though his mom had said his dad was going to be okay, Marty had been terrified that whole drive home from Santa Barbara two weeks ago. His dad had gotten caught on the wrong side of a black bear and her two cubs when a ranch guest—who thought he knew more about ranching than Buck from watching *Cowboy Country* on TV every weekend—took off in chase of a stray. Turned out the guest had less than stellar distance vision, and the stray cow had actually been a bear. In forcing a safe distance between bear and guest, Buck's horse had spooked and thrown him off.

Fortunately, he'd been knocked unconscious from the fall, and the bear had left him alone. Unfortunately, he'd landed badly on his now broken collarbone.

A man like Buck Fairgrave didn't do laid-up well, so Marty found himself spending more time trying to keep Buck in the house and out of trouble than actually getting his work done.

"You behave yourself, Dad." Marty placed his glass on the table between them and stepped down off the veranda to greet Tripp.

Wild horses couldn't stop the smile that stretched across his face when Tripp exited the truck with an answering smile of his own.

They had talked on the phone a few times since he'd left the circuit to help while his dad healed—about Buck, Marty's days on the ranch, Tripp's rides, and latest happenings on the circuit—but neither had broached the one subject most in need of discussion. As far as Marty had been able to tell, Tripp had shoved the whole thing to the back of his closet again—as if "out of sight, out of mind" was an acceptable solution.

But seeing Tripp in person again pushed all that aside and sent a rush of heat skittering southward. That immediate reaction to Tripp never seemed to lessen, only grew stronger every time he saw him.

Marty began to lift his arms for a welcoming hug, but when Tripp's eyes darted sideways, to where Buck sat watching them intently from the porch, he shoved his hands into his pockets. Tripp did the same, whether he realized it or not, but Marty didn't call him on it. He knew better. It was hard to swallow, but this was the same old Tripp.

"Hey," Tripp said.

"Hey back."

"Can we . . . uh." Tripp's gaze flitted beyond Marty and then back. "Can we talk?"

"Sure." He didn't move. Tripp gestured toward the pasture with a tilt of his head and raised an eyebrow, but Marty decided to test him a little. "But first come meet my dad."

Tripp paled ever so slightly, but nodded. As they turned to walk to the deck shoulder to shoulder, Marty slanted a sideways glance at him. "Relax. My family knows about us."

Tripp stumbled, but quickly recovered and kept on walking.

They climbed the steps, and his dad stood. Out of the corner of his eye, Marty watched Tripp's Adam's apple bob in a nervous swallow.

Even with his arm encased in fiberglass from fingers to shoulder and braced in an awkward position, Buck could still stop a bull in its tracks with one threatening glare.

"Dad, I'd like you to meet Tripp Colby." Marty shot a silent warning at his dad to be on his best behavior. "Tripp, this is my dad, Buck Fairgrave."

Tripp cleared his throat and stepped forward, extending his hand. "Pleasure to meet you, sir. Was real sorry to hear about the accident."

Buck nodded and took the proffered hand in what Marty knew would be a more than firm grip, but he kept the tone of his voice friendly. "Nice to meet you. And the name's Buck, not sir."

Tripp tipped his head in acknowledgment and stepped back.

"Okay." Marty collected his phone from the table and shoved it in his back pocket. "I'm going to show Tripp the grounds. You got everything you need?"

"I'm not an invalid, son. Anything I don't got now I can get for m'self later."

Marty smiled at his stubborn old man.

"And, Tripp?" Buck narrowed his eyes and lowered his voice. "Don't let the cast fool you. Hurt my boy again, and I will take your skinny ass down faster than you can say eight seconds."

"Dad." A flush of heat raced up Marty's neck and into his cheeks.

"No, it's okay." Tripp's hand ghosted over Marty's elbow in a placating gesture, and the near-PDA shocked him so much he barely heard Tripp continue. "That's the last thing I ever intend to do. You have my word on it."

Buck nodded. A man's word and a spit-shake were as legally binding to his dad as any five-hundred-page contract signed in triplicate.

Marty shot another heatless glare over his shoulder at Buck as he and Tripp walked away. His dad smirked back proudly, returning to his chair to hold court over his domain. Marty shook his head. *God love him.*

"Your dad's a piece of work," Tripp said as Marty led him along a worn path toward a large paddock near the smaller of two barns, where several horses grazed. They stepped up to the wooden fencing, and in a pose synonymous with the essential nature of the cowboy, both hooked a boot on the lower rung and leaned over their forearms on the top rail. They stood close enough for Tripp's shoulder to brush against Marty's, and a painful longing spread into his chest. Even though his knee-jerk reaction was to move away and put an acceptable distance between them, the need to feel Marty, to touch and be close to him, kept Tripp right where he was.

A stocky palomino sauntered over to investigate them. Finding no carrots, apples, or even sugar cubes on offer, he snorted and, with a haughty swish of his tail, wandered back to resume grazing.

The lazy afternoon buzzed around them, and a sense of peace settled over him. Grateful for Marty's easy way, he let himself relax into the mood of the ranch before getting into what had made him drive all the way from San Dimas, when it hit him. He had a small house with a few acres in Modesto, but this was the kind of spread he'd like for his own when it came time to hang up his spurs. The man at his side was the one he wanted to share it with.

Knowing the silence between them would continue until he broke it, Tripp swallowed his pride and, keeping his gaze on the horses, said what he'd come to say: "I've missed you."

In his peripheral vision, he saw Marty turn toward him, feeling more than seeing the smile that lit Marty's handsome face.

"I've missed you, too."

Tripp turned to Marty and sank into those warm hazel eyes. Eyes that saw more in him than he'd ever seen in himself.

"I want you back."

Marty regarded him for a long moment. The warmth in his expression didn't change, but the gold flecks of his irises somehow darkened to more of a bronze. "Have you cleared the way for me?"

Tripp frowned, and Marty sighed. By unspoken mutual agreement, they both turned to stare out at the pasture. The horses had moved farther away, the occasional snort added accent to the quiet drone of bees seeking nectar in a nearby bushel of lavender.

"Please, Marty." Tripp tried to remain steady, not give away how desperately he needed Marty. But he *was* desperate and couldn't prevent it from coloring his tone. "I want to, but I can't do this alone. Not yet. I need you there with me."

"In your closet?"

"Just until the season ends, until the World Championships in Vegas."

"And what comes after that?"

"What do you mean, after that?"

"You know what I mean. First it's the Worlds, then it'll be after the promo tour, then after . . ." Marty swatted at a fly and turned to Tripp. "There'll always be a reason to put it off."

"Christ, Marty." He stepped back from the fence. Hooves pounded in the distance. Real or imagined, he couldn't be sure. "I can't pencil in a day on the calendar to officially come out."

"I'm not asking you to come out."

"Yes! You are!"

Marty glared with eyes almost solid dark green now, lips pressed tight together in clear effort to hold in check whatever he'd been about to say. He took a slow breath. "I am *not* asking you to come out. I *am* asking you to deal with your past and make peace with it. Whether you decide to come out or not is beside the point."

His tone was so reasonable and his cadence so calculated that it set off all of Tripp's defense mechanisms. He checked his own voice, making sure not to raise it again, but still the words tumbled out in a barely controlled growl. "Then what the fuck is the point? Do you want me out of the closet or not?"

Marty closed his eyes. When he opened them and looked down at Tripp, *into* him, Tripp saw sadness so deep that it felt like a railway spike driving through his chest.

"I want you to be happy."

"Then come back to me."

Marty's mouth lifted into a crooked, forlorn smile. He raised a hand and cupped Tripp's jaw. Tripp closed his eyes and leaned into the touch. Melted into it. Why did he have to deal with all that shit? It was so fucking . . . exhausting. Ancient history best left buried and forgotten.

"You need to make peace with yourself first," Marty whispered.

"I can't do it without you."

"Look at me."

He opened his eyes, but unable to meet Marty's, he focused on the horses in the distance. He was losing Marty. Losing the only thing he'd found to give him a reason for being.

"*Look* at me, Tripp." A command this time.

When he acquiesced, Marty slipped his hand to the back of Tripp's neck and squeezed, holding him firm.

"You are stronger than you believe. You are the strongest man I've ever known, and I know you can do this. You *will* do this. Do you hear me?" He gave Tripp a little shake for emphasis, waiting until Tripp acknowledged him with a quick nod before continuing. "I can't hide in your closet with you so you can ignore your fears. You know that. Face them down once and for all, and send them running with their tails between their legs, because if you don't confront them, you will always be under their control. How can we ever have a healthy relationship with them always breathing over our shoulders and ultimately running the show?"

Marty dipped down so the brims of their hats tapped. Tripp angled up for a kiss, but Marty stepped back, and the hand fell from his neck, leaving a chill in its place. The cold spread until his throat froze shut and his heart stopped beating. A wave of dizziness spun the world before him, and he had to close his eyes so as not to fall over.

Somewhere in the distance he heard the soft timbre of Marty's voice. "I know you can do this." But it didn't quite register. All he could focus on was how Marty had just drawn the boundary lines between them. Lines that grew thicker with each step on their silent walk back to Tripp's truck.

Tripp absently offered up a wave and weak smile for Buck when they passed the house, then stopped and took a long look at Marty. He catalogued everything about the man, from his well-worn Wranglers with frayed hems that bunched over dusty working boots, to a red chambray shirt, and a straw-colored cowboy hat with a braided brown leather band. His dark hair curled at the ends just over his collar, and the easy smile that had first drawn Tripp to the tall, unassuming cowboy reflected in kind eyes.

I will erase these lines. I will not lose you.

Marty stepped forward and wrapped Tripp in his arms. The one place Tripp wanted to be so badly that even knowing they had an audience didn't faze him. He held on tighter and memorized the way their bodies fit perfectly together, how good it felt simply to hold and be held by Marty.

"I'm here if you need me." Marty disengaged himself from the embrace. "As your friend."

Chapter Eleven

Three days later, Tripp found himself in the last place he'd ever thought he'd be: sitting alone at a café in San Francisco's Castro district.

"Relax, sweetheart." The waiter refilled his coffee. "No one's going to hassle you here."

Tripp shifted in his seat, even more uncomfortable than when he'd first arrived. "That obvious, am I?"

The waiter offered a kind smile and moved on to the next table. Tripp sighed and looked down at his coffee. He had tried not to stand out, but he couldn't dress any way other than cowboy and felt naked without his hat. Which seemed to earn him more attention than the drag queens strutting down the boulevard in their thigh-high platform boots, miniskirts, and brightly colored feather boas. He'd dodged their wolf whistles and attempts to lure him across the street and made quick work of ducking inside the café, where he was now waiting for a date with his past.

All the while praying to God that Marty knew what he was talking about.

When he'd left Marty's ranch earlier in the week, he knew exactly what he had to do to get his cowboy back. With his mission firmly in mind, he stopped at the Bridgeport Library and headed straight to its single public computer, where he began researching the whereabouts of a hopefully still living Timothy Moore.

He'd been a little skeptical initially when Timothy's name came up on the first search page, linked to a place called *The Beacon* in San Francisco—an outreach center with housing, counseling, and career development for homeless and troubled LGBT youths. He didn't think it could be that easy, but he'd dialed the phone number with shaking hands and held his breath. After an extended moment of stunned silence when he asked if the man on the other end of the line was the same boy who'd grown up in Winston-Salem, North Carolina, more than twenty years ago, he'd realized maybe some things in life could be that easy.

The front doors of the café opened, and two men entered. Both wore jeans and matching polo shirts, sported the requisite golden California tans, and on their feet . . . flip-flops. The shorter of the two had hair the color of straw with long bangs that flopped over one eye; the other man was also blond, but a darker shade styled more conservatively. They made an attractive couple. The shorter man turned, and his eyes immediately locked on Tripp. He sucked in a breath and held it. After so many years it was hard to remember what Timothy had looked like, but he knew he was looking at the grown-up version now.

Then Timothy smiled—a bright, genuine smile that lit up his face and about knocked Tripp out of his seat. Timothy grabbed the other man's hand, and the two approached. That open, friendly expression didn't change, and Tripp found himself feeling out of his depth. He hadn't expected to see such a clearly happy person, but then, he hadn't known what to expect. Not really. Not beyond every possible worst-case scenario his guilty conscience could create to torture him with for years on end.

"Tripp Colby." The voice was deep, the words soft-spoken. "As I live and breathe."

"Timothy Moore."

Timothy's expression brightened. "That would be *Everson-Moore* now."

Remembering his manners, Tripp stood up and extended his hand in greeting. Timothy let go of his partner and pulled Tripp into a solid hug. Then he stepped back, but didn't let go. Holding onto Tripp's biceps, he did a head-to-toe perusal. "Aren't you a sight for sore eyes, cowboy."

When the man standing behind Timothy cleared his throat, Timothy rolled his eyes playfully, gave Tripp's arms a squeeze, and let go.

"Tripp, this is my husband, David Everson-Moore. David, my old friend from high school, Tripp Colby, three-time professional bull riding world champion."

Tripp raised his eyebrows, and a pink blush colored Timothy's cheeks. "I Googled you after your call the other day."

"It's nice to meet a real live cowboy." David clasped his hand in a firm grip, the smile as friendly and welcoming as Timothy's.

"A pleasure." Tripp said with a tip of his hat.

It wasn't until Timothy and David were sitting beside each other across the table from him that he noticed the logo on their matching shirts: written in an arc over a rainbow, it read *The Beacon*. So they ran the center together. Tripp wondered if that was how they'd met.

"Wow." Timothy leaned back. "Tripp Colby. I don't even know where to begin."

Tripp knew where to begin, but he hadn't planned on having company for the conversation. He reached for a sugar packet sitting beside his cup and began rolling one of the corners between his thumb and forefinger. He cleared his throat. "About that. I actually had something specific I wanted to talk about. To ask you."

Timothy leveled an assessing gaze on him. Long enough that Tripp had to fight the urge to squirm in his seat. "David, honey. Do you mind getting me an iced tea and one of those marshmallow treats?"

"Sure thing, baby." David kissed Timothy's temple and excused himself from the table. Timothy watched him walk away with a dreamy smile.

"How long have you two been together?" Tripp stalled. He could feel the topic burning a hole in his guts, trying to force its way out. That or he'd drunk too much coffee.

Timothy's smile widened, and his blue eyes danced. "Thirteen years now. We met at a Pride party, got to talking, one thing led to another, and next thing you know..." Timothy lifted his left hand and waggled his fingers. The gold band flashed in the light.

"That's really great to hear. I'm glad things have worked out so well for you." And he meant it, but so far this mission of his hadn't garnered any big epiphany. Or relief. Or bright light showing him the way to freedom . . . or whatever the hell was supposed to happen.

"Not what you expected though, is it?"

Timothy seemed so carefree and unassuming at first, but Tripp was quickly coming to realize that not much missed the man's notice. Clearly running a center for gay teens was his calling. Tripp dropped the now mangled sugar packet to the table and shoved it aside.

"I didn't really know what to expect, honestly. I guess I needed to know that you were okay. After . . . after what happened."

Timothy's eyes held his until Tripp's fears began to creep up his spine. Sharp, cold fingers dug into his skin.

"I won't deny it was the most horrible experience of my life." Timothy glanced out the window, his gaze briefly turning inward. "But it made me stronger than I could have ever imagined. I won't go into details. I've spent my time in therapy dealing with what the center did to me. I've dealt with it, learned from it, and put it behind me. I'll never forget, but it doesn't have any power over me anymore."

Just like that? The question was on the tip of Tripp's tongue, but he couldn't voice it. Of course it hadn't been "just like that." But still, Timothy had shed his past and moved on to a seemingly wonderful life. A whisper of hope breezed through his mind.

"What I will tell you is that my time there showed me who I really was. How much I loved that person, and I fought for him tooth and nail. They couldn't fix what wasn't wrong, and I sure as hell wasn't going to let them break me. No matter how hard they tried. Finally, they decided I was too far gone to be saved, and I was released."

A small smile touched Timothy's lips, but for the first time since sitting down, Tripp noticed it didn't reach his eyes.

"My parents weren't there to pick me up. No one was there. So I went straight to the bank where I had a small savings and cleared out my account, then I stuck out my thumb and hitched across the country. I've been in San Francisco ever since. I found my salvation right here."

Tripp stared across the table in awe, humbled and speechless by how certain Timothy was of himself—even as a teenager. Timothy refused to let the shit life threw at him stick and instead tossed it right back. Tripp may have a dangerous career that gave people the impression he was fearless, but Timothy Moore . . . this bright, intelligent, friendly, generous man was the true hero. He had real courage.

For the first time since his father had found that magazine, Tripp understood what it meant to be true to oneself, and just maybe that was the epiphany he'd been looking for all along.

"God, Timothy. I'm so sorry. Can you ever forgive me?" The words spilled from his mouth, and he placed both hands flat on the table, as if that would keep him from spilling out of his skin along with them.

Timothy frowned. "What on earth for?"

Tripp ran a hand over his face and looked out the window. "I'm the reason you were sent to the center in the first place. I . . . outed you."

Timothy leaned back in his chair and regarded Tripp with an intensity he couldn't bear to look in the face. There it was. The real Tripp Colby was a coward. Timothy still hadn't said a word in response, and Tripp's heart pounded so hard and fast it sounded like galloping hoof beats.

The gentle weight of a hand on his drew his attention back to the man across the table. Tripp couldn't accept the concern he saw there and dropped his gaze to the smaller hand holding his. The skin was smooth, soft. Not the rough, callused hands of men who worked ranches and rodeos.

"Please tell me you haven't been carrying this on your shoulders all this time." A touch of distress colored Timothy's voice.

Tripp couldn't look up into those too-kind eyes, couldn't speak through the constriction of his throat, so he nodded. One curt tip of his head.

"Oh, Tripp." Timothy reached out with his other hand to cup Tripp's in both of his. "You were never to blame. We were kids, and kids are reactionary by nature. If there's anyone to blame, it's my parents. They were the adults who should have known better. They should have loved me unconditionally. Which is one of the reasons why David and I started The Beacon. For all those kids whose parents can't accept their own children."

Tripp's throat grew tighter, and his vision began to blur. *Oh, hell no. This is not happening.* He squeezed his eyes shut and pinched the bridge of his nose with his free hand until he was confident he had a grip on himself.

Timothy dipped his head and lowered his voice. "You aren't out, are you?"

Tripp shook his head, afraid to try his voice just yet.

"Is there someone in your life?"

At the thought of Marty, Tripp not only nodded but also smiled, and a short laugh bubbled up from his chest. "Yes," he said, his voice ragged. "In a way, he sent me to you. Said I needed to make peace with my past before we could move forward. Too many people in my closet, apparently."

Timothy nodded. "Sounds like a smart man. I'd love to meet him some day."

"I'd like that."

Timothy gave his hand a squeeze and then let go. "What happened all those years ago, it wasn't your fault, and it was never your burden to bear. My life has been good. Better than good. I couldn't have asked for more. I have a wonderful man who's shown me the true meaning of love. I have a rewarding career helping others find their own way. I have no regrets and no complaints. So please, for your sake, for the sake of that man out there who obviously loves you enough to know what you need most, let go. You never needed to carry this."

That was it. Tripp couldn't hold back anymore. He jumped from his chair and pulled a startled Timothy into his arms. He held on so tightly the poor man gasped for breath but didn't complain. Hands settled on Tripp's back and moved in slow circles as he cried silently into Timothy's shoulder.

When the dust settled from the stampede that had shaken him to his core, he finally released Timothy. He wiped his eyes and started to laugh. Not only had he hugged another man in public, he'd cried like a baby, and the earth hadn't opened up and swallowed him whole.

"You're going to be okay. The first step is the hardest. It won't always be easy, but it does get better from here on out."

Tripp smiled at the sincerity in Timothy's words and their reflection in his kind eyes. Life had definitely gotten better for Timothy, so why couldn't it get better for him as well? He had no doubt there would be hard times ahead, especially once word got out on the circuit. To Scott. A chill whispered over his skin, but he pushed the thought away before it could sink deeper. Just knowing he hadn't completely destroyed Timothy's life went a long way toward making this new road he'd turned onto easier to navigate. He wasn't sure he was ready to take the seatbelt off just yet, but at least he had the right map now.

"Thank you." Tripp wrapped his arms around Timothy again, releasing him quickly. "Thank you."

David moved up next to Timothy, put an arm over his shoulder, and pulled him close to his side. "Everyone okay?"

Timothy and Tripp nodded in unison, and Tripp said, "Better than."

After giving Timothy one more hug, and David too, on the sidewalk in front of the café, they parted ways with promises to keep in touch and open invites to stay at each other's homes when visiting.

Tripp walked down the street toward the lot where he'd left his truck, a timid smile threatening to stretch his lips. The extended stares of open admiration he received from the men he passed were like little badges of approval, filling up his shaky well of confidence even as he struggled to meet their gazes.

It was so damned cliché, but the release from guilt Timothy had given him lifted a weight from his shoulders, from his heart and mind, and his feet didn't seem to strike the pavement quite as heavily as they used to. Emboldened by this newfound taste of freedom, he walked through the doors of the next establishment he came to. He didn't even notice what kind of store it was, but it didn't matter. He wasn't there to shop.

He strolled right up to the clerk with such forced determination that the poor man's eyes widened and he took a step back. Tripp smiled, hoping it was big enough, genuine enough, to ease the startled clerk. He struck out his hand... and promptly froze.

Oh, my God. What am I doing? His fledgling resolve began a swift retreat. Cold perspiration crept up the back of his neck, and his pulse pounded in his ears, and all the while his trembling hand hung suspended in space. The clerk raised a manicured eyebrow, and Tripp swallowed. Hard.

I can do this. IcanIcanIcan.

With effort, he reined in his fortitude before attempting to escape with it out the door.

"Hi-i." His voice squeaked, and curiosity flickered in the clerk's makeup enhanced eyes. Tripp cleared his throat. "Hi, I'm Tripp. Tripp Colby."

The clerk, whose nametag read Jamie, looked from Tripp's hand to his face and then, deciding to play along with the strange, stuttering man in his store, reached out and shook Tripp's hand, his grip warm and firm.

"Hi there, Tripp." There was a note of amusement in his voice. "I'm Jamie."

Tripp nodded. He pushed as much confidence as he could muster into his voice, but still heard an edge of fear in it. "I'm... uh..." He took a deep breath, exhaled slowly, then met Jamie's stare. "I'm gay."

There. Done. He knew it was cheating for his first public announcement to be in a place guaranteed to accept it, but good God did it feel good. Liberating. Empowering. He could do this. Marty was right. The little breeze of hope he'd felt in the café increased to a strong wind.

"Well, you're in the right neighborhood, honey." Jamie ran his gaze over Tripp, pausing for a lingering stare at his crotch. "Nice buckle. I'm sure you know the saying, save a horse and all that. I'll be your horse anytime. You can leave your hat on. Boots too."

Tripp started laughing, but quickly reined it in, holding up a hand at the offended expression on Jamie's face. "Thank you. Really. I am flattered, but I'm taken. At least, I hope I am. If he'll take me back."

Jamie relaxed, eyes sparkling, and he licked his lips. "I honestly can't imagine why he wouldn't. Gorgeous hunk o' cowboy like you?" Jamie shook his head, grinning.

The earlier light gust of hope escalated into a full-fledge hurricane. He needed to call Marty and hear his voice, tell him he was clearing the way with a damn bulldozer.

"I have to go." He reached for Jamie's hand, but Jaime pulled him into a quick hug. Jamie smiled and Tripp nodded, his mission there accomplished and successful, and nothing more needed to be said. He turned for the exit, using every ounce of his restraint to keep from sprinting all the way to his truck, all the while praying Marty would take him back.

Chapter Twelve

By the time Tripp pulled into the Industry Hills rodeo grounds late the next afternoon, the bulldozer had morphed into a push lawn mower. What had seemed like a good idea at the time now had him breaking out into a cold sweat, white-knuckling the steering wheel of his truck, and made his boots heavy with concrete.

Not planning to stay on the grounds overnight, he parked as close as possible to the exit gate instead of going into the competitor camping area. He killed the engine and sat for a moment to psych himself up. The spectator crowd had begun to thin out since the day's last events had already wrapped. Cowboys and cowgirls led their horses to a bath station at one end of a lean-to style barn, taking turns hosing their animals down and readying them to settle in for the night.

He'd been riding so high on the whirlwind of freedom after his meeting with Timothy that he'd made a phone call that had led to an impromptu meeting in Los Angeles that in turn had meant missing the first day of the last rodeo on the regular California circuit. Not making today's rides wouldn't have any effect on his standings, and it wasn't like he needed the prize money, but that wasn't his concern just now.

Taking another fortifying breath, Tripp exited the truck, adjusted his hat a little lower over his brow, and made his way across the grounds to the big equine RV that Bridge Sullivan and Kent Murphy shared.

When he rounded the rig, he saw Eric setting out three patio chairs by a cooler Tripp knew would be full of cold beers. Bridge was setting up a table on the other side of a fire pit for their regular post-rodeo poker game, and Kent was nowhere to be seen.

Bridge furrowed his eyebrows and frowned, stepping around the table and toward Tripp.

"Marty ain't here." His tone was hard, his hands on his hips.

Eric looked from Bridge to Tripp and back, then sat down in his chair and cracked his beer, watching with open curiosity as if Bridge and Tripp were a couple of rodeo clowns about to put on a show.

Tripp took a step closer so their voices wouldn't carry. He shoved his hands into his pockets, hiding them so they wouldn't give away the shake that thrummed steadily through him.

"I know. I'm here to talk to you and Kent." He bit back his pride. "And Eric."

Bridge remained where he was, his expression unchanging, but Tripp didn't miss the flash of interest in his eyes. Bridge crossed his arms, and without breaking eye contact, shouted over his shoulder.

"Yo, Kent. Get your skinny ass out here!"

A long few seconds later, the door to the mobile home opened, and Kent stepped down. He looked like he'd been about to crack some joke in response to Bridge, but his expression vanished like a slate wiped clean when he saw Tripp.

"Marty's not here." Different voice, same imposing tone.

"Yeah, got that already." Tripp immediately regretted the spike of sarcasm in his voice. He didn't want to put these guys on the offensive any more than they already were. He huffed out a breath. "Listen," he began in a placating tone. "I don't want there to be any animosity between us all, for Marty's sake if nothing else."

"And why is that?" Kent stepped up beside Bridge and crossed his arms over his chest in a mirror image.

Tripp shifted on his feet and squared his shoulders. "Because I plan on spending a lot more time with him, which by default means spending more time with you guys, so I'd appreciate it if we could all at least be civil."

Bridge snorted. "Mighty big of you. But what the hell is this all about?"

Tripp took a quick scan of the grounds—no one appeared to be within earshot, and a few rigs beginning to roll out offered suitable sound interference.

He turned back to three sets of curious eyes trained on him, two of which seemed to be losing patience.

Tripp looked down at his boots for a second, gulped in a mouthful of dusty air while listening for the sound of galloping hoof beats. But they didn't come. Over the too fast thudding of his own heartbeat, all he heard were the comforting sounds of rodeo life going on about its business. He lifted his gaze to the three men, meeting each of theirs. "I'm gay."

All three expressions remained the same. Tripp cleared his throat. "I've been seeing Marty in secret for over a year, but now I'm coming out. We'll be out. Together. And I-I just thought you guys should know. I'll be around more. I—"

He was babbling. He didn't do babbling. *Just shut up already.*

The din of activity around them grew louder. A light sheen of perspiration broke out over his skin, and he fought the urge to take off his hat and wipe his forehead. Perhaps this hadn't been his best idea after all. Even still, he knew in his guts it was right. He stood his ground, stood taller. Fuck them. He'd already faced down his biggest demon and won. He'd taken further steps to overcome them in the intervening hours, and each time he'd come out unscathed and that much stronger.

And come hell or high water, he *would* get Marty back, whether these cowboys accepted him or not.

"And in other breaking news . . ." Bridge finally said. "You want a gold star now?"

"Bridge." Eric shot a disapproving glare at him. "Give the man a break. It's not easy what he just did."

Bridge shrugged, reached into the cooler for a couple cans of beer. "Don't see any reason why we should. Dude's been a prick to Marty for too long to get off that easy."

"Y'all knew?" Tripp wasn't quite sure how to process that. Marty had never said anything. No one had, and Tripp had always thought the only reason the two men had such a hate-on for him was because he was friends with Scott, not because he'd been keeping Marty in his closet.

"We're his best friends, man." Kent deftly caught the can Bridge tossed his way. "What do you think?"

"You two I get." Tripp inclined his head toward Eric. "But him?"

Eric tapped the side of his head with a finger and smirked. "Top-of-the-line gaydar."

Tripp stared at him, shook his head, and turned back to the other two. "Thank you for not saying anything."

"Don't flatter yourself, sweetheart." Bridge popped his beer tab and took a swig. "We sure as hell didn't keep mum for you."

Tripp nodded. "Just the same."

"Well," Bridge said. "If you're truly legit about this, then prove it."

Eric angled sideways in his chair. "Bridge—"

"No. Bridge is right," Kent said. "Words are cheap. If he's serious, then he needs to back it up with real action."

Eric shook his head and stood up. "No, he doesn't. You two have no idea what it takes to do what he just did. That right there was the *real action*."

He lifted the lid of the cooler, pulled out a can, and approached Tripp. He extended his right hand.

"Ignore them. I for one am impressed you found the courage to take that step. The world's a lot brighter when you're good with who you are."

Tripp looked from the sincere smile on Eric's face down to his hand. He accepted it for a three-beat shake. "'ppreciate it." He swallowed back a lump in his throat. "Thank you."

Eric nodded, then handed him the beer.

"Oh, and fair warning." His voice pitched an octave lower. "Fuck up again and I'll be there to pick up the pieces."

Tripp glared hard at Eric, his hackles rising. Eric laughed and smacked him on the biceps.

"Good! That's what I was hoping to see."

Eric sat back down and smiled up at Tripp, clearly pleased with himself. Tripp wasn't quite sure what to make of Eric yet, but he did know the man would not be taking Marty from him. Ever.

"Thanks for this." Tripp lifted the beer and placed it back inside the cooler. "And thank you hearing me out, but I have a few things I need to do tonight."

Three heads nodded in unison, and just before Tripp turned to leave, he looked to Kent and Bridge.

"Be sure and check out PBR's website tomorrow for your proof."

"There you are!" Lily stood in the doorway of the mudroom with her face scrunched up. Marty tried not to groan and hooked his right boot heel into the bootjack by the door to extricate his foot.

"What's going on?" He wedged his left foot into the jack.

"Your friends!" Lily rolled her eyes. "The dynamic duo have been taking turns driving me up the wall, calling all day looking for you."

"On the house line? Why didn't they call my cell?"

"Probably because you haven't been answering the damn thing, why do you think?"

Marty shook his head and reached into his back jeans pocket, only to come up empty. "Shit."

He closed his eyes and tried to visualize where he'd seen it last. "I think I left it in the tack room the other day."

He'd taken it out wanting to call Tripp, but had been interrupted by one of their guests. He didn't remember going back for it, which meant it still had to be there—and completely dead by now.

"Way to go, Smarts." Lily shook her head and laughed before disappearing into the house.

Marty followed her inside and poured a huge glass of iced tea before picking up the cordless handset. He leaned against the counter and punched in Bridge's number.

"Dude!" Marty winced and held the phone away from his ear. "Where the hell have you been, and why aren't you answering your fucking phone?"

"I left it in the barn. It's probably dead."

"Well go get it and plug the fucker in!"

"Thanks for the tip, Einstein." Marty picked up his tea and took a long draught. "What the hell's on fire?"

"Your damn boyfriend."

Marty straightened up so fast he just about dropped his glass to the floor. "What about him? Is he okay? What happened?"

"Chill, man. He's fine. Impressed the fuck out of me and Kent this morning."

"Tell him about yesterday." Kent's voice came through in the background.

"What about yesterday? What did he do?" The excitement in his friends' voices echoed in his chest.

Bridge laughed.

"Log on to the PBR website. You can't miss it."

"Okay." Marty headed for the computer in the den at the back of the house. "I'm going."

"Good. I gotta bolt," Bridge said. "I'll catch ya at the banquet tomorrow night."

"See ya." Marty disconnected and dropped the phone on the desk. Still standing, he logged on and waited for the page to load. Front and center popped up a "breaking news" splash bar announcing an exclusive interview with Tripp Colby. Marty clicked on the link, the page loaded, he read the headline...

And fell blindly into the chair behind him when his legs gave out.

"Holy. Shit."

Marty squeezed his eyes shut and then looked again. He blinked. Still the same. He read it twice more to be certain:

TRIPP COLBY PAINTS THE CHUTE WITH RAINBOW COLORS
Three-time professional bull riding champion comes out, drops homophobic sponsor

> LOS ANGELES, Calif. — Tripp Colby, three-time World Champion, blew the chute wide open Saturday morning when in an exclusive interview, he announced he had dropped his long-time major sponsor, Jackson Motors, citing "irrevocable differences regarding equality and human rights." He went further to call out the dealership as not only homophobic, but also as staunch supporters of controversial conversion therapy centers that promise to "cure" homosexuality. Colby claims Jackson Motors owner Darren Jackson was the co-owner of such a center in Winston-Salem, North Carolina, up until four years ago, when the center was forced to close due to public pressure regarding its extreme aversion techniques.

Marty's hand shook on the mouse as he scrolled slowly down the page. The article went on to explain a brief history and the current debates regarding conversion therapy camps, which he skimmed. He continued reading:

> Colby, now 33 years old, said it was time to come out and live honestly. That just might be harder than riding 2,000-pound bulls for a living in a sport historically associated with super macho, rough and tough men of the Wild West. Colby, one of the sport's most high-profile riders, is now breaking stereotypes and has set himself up to be a role model for gay athletes by publicly coming out while still actively competing.
>
> "The support I've received so far has been positive," Colby said.
>
> When asked if Colby had someone special in his life, he confirmed having been in a relationship with another man but refused any further details.

When he reached the end of the article, he scrolled up to the top of the page and read the whole thing again. He sat back in the chair and smiled. Admiration and fierce love for Tripp lifted his heart. He'd known Tripp could face his demons and beat them, but he never would have expected this. To come out publicly on the PBR website? That was going to...

He sat back up and clicked onto *RodeoBoards*, scrolling quickly through recent comments. As he thought, the news had gone viral.

He smacked his hand on the desk and jumped up. "He did it! Oh my God, he did it."

Chapter Thirteen

Marty scanned the faces in the crowd for one in particular, but coming up empty, he made a beeline across the packed hall to where his friends were gathered near a buffet table.

"Have you guys seen Tripp?"

Bridge frowned. "Not since after the rodeo yesterday."

"Yeah, he came by for the usual thanks." Kent nodded. "Even stuck around and played a quick hand of poker with us. But I haven't seen him since."

Marty looked to Eric, who just shook his head.

A trickle of worry threaded down Marty's spine. He hadn't been able to reach Tripp since he'd read the article. After he'd found his cell phone and recharged it, there'd been a couple of short messages from Tripp on Saturday. In the first, Tripp had said he had news to share but didn't want to do it over the phone. The tone of his voice had been so light and carefree that Marty almost hadn't recognized it. In the second, Tripp said he just wanted to hear Marty's voice, which had sent a rush of warmth cascading through his chest. Neither message had given him any cause for concern.

He pulled his phone out and tried again, but the call went directly to voicemail. He disconnected but stared hard at the phone, as if he could will it to ring. Something was definitely not right. Tripp always had his phone on him when he wasn't competing, and he always returned his calls.

"What's going on?" Kent stepped forward, concern reflected in his eyes.

Marty shook his head and did another scan of the crowd, spotting his least favorite person by the bar. He shouldered his way through the crush of bodies until he was standing next to

Scott, who shot a disdainful sideways glance at him and then resumed watching over the festivities like some sort of high-court lord.

Clear that he would get no further acknowledgment, Marty cut right to the chase. "Where's Tripp?"

Scott didn't so much as twitch, and continued to stare somewhere across the room. Marty shifted around to stand directly in front of Scott. He was a good four inches or so taller, which had Scott looking at his chin for a long moment before finally raising his gaze to meet Marty's. Dark eyes bore into Marty with contempt so deep and barely restrained that he had to resist the urge to take a step backward.

"Like I should give a flying fuck?" The venom in Scott's voice wasn't lessened by the slight slur of his words, and sent a shiver down Marty's back. All of his senses screamed, "Run!" But he stood his ground.

"Can you stop being an asshole for half a minute and tell me where I can find Tripp?"

Scott pushed away from the wall, putting him close enough for Marty to smell the man's breath. Fresh hops with a bitter undertone.

"What the fuck do you care?"

"I just need to know where he is."

It was then that Marty noticed the whites of Scott's eyes were bloodshot. Behind the hatred and aggression they appeared rattled, frenetic . . . even haunted. Deep purple crescents hung underneath. Something heavy was going on with the man. Anyone else he would have reached out to, but not Scott Gillard. Right now he didn't give a rat's ass what Scott's issues were. He just needed to find Tripp.

The light in Scott's eyes shifted, the expression on his face twisted, and his mouth stretched into a disconcerting smile.

"Oh, I get it." His tone was low and menacing. "You got a thing for that yellow-bellied faggot."

Marty's stomach knotted, and a cold wave washed over his skin.

"You're one of his butt buddies, aren't you?"

Scott had never held back expressing his disgust for gay men and, with a hair-trigger temper, had always been quick to fight. It was clear that the cowboy had read Tripp's PBR interview, and knowing Scott, he'd probably completely lost his shit and left a path of destruction a mile wide in his wake. That a friend of *his* should turn out to be gay . . .

"And you thought he was coming out for you, did you? Oh, poor pretty little Marty. Your hero ran off with another man even prettier. He's gone and he ain't never coming back. Good fucking riddance."

Scott may as well have punched him in the solar plexus. A wave of dizziness rocked him on his heels, but he managed to stay upright.

"You're a liar." His voice sounded distant and weak to his own ears.

Scott growled. "You need to get the fuck out of my face right now before I break yours in half."

"You need help, Scott. You really do." Marty realized that probably had not been the wisest thing to say. Not to this particular man, and especially not in his present state. He may as well have just tried to yank a fresh bone from the jaws of a pit bull.

Scott raised fists and took a step forward. Marty did step backward then, but instead of finding empty space to run for safety, his retreat was thwarted by a wall of solid flesh.

Cornered.

For a second he thought the men surrounding him were Scott's crew and he was in for the bashing of his lifetime, but before panic could take hold, Kent moved up to stand at his left side while Bridge and Eric flanked his right.

Scott stopped and made eye contact with each of them, as if mentally marking them. He lowered his hands but didn't unclench them.

"The lot of you make me sick." He spat, and Marty felt the warm spittle trickle down his cheek. Scott forced his way between Marty and Bridge, knocking them both off balance, and stormed from the hall, shoving people out of his way as he went.

"You okay?" Eric put a hand on Marty's shoulder.

Unable to find words, Marty just nodded. Shaken, but okay.

He took a trembling breath and looked at his friends. "I think Scott did something to Tripp."

A week later, Marty still hadn't heard from Tripp. All his calls and messages had gone unanswered and unreturned. Fearing that Scott and Tripp had gotten into a fight and Tripp had been injured, he'd called every hospital between Industry and Modesto, but no Tripp Colbys had been admitted. He even checked the morgues, his breath shallow and heart pounding every time he inquired, the relief at receiving a negative answer leaving him dizzy with hope. Somewhere out there, Tripp was still alive. So why was Tripp avoiding him?

With the regular season over and another three weeks before the World Championships in Vegas, Tripp wasn't due anywhere until then. Without anyone expecting him, there wasn't anyone to worry about his absence.

Except for Marty. He'd hardly eaten all week. His mom had managed to force a few bowls of soup down his throat, but even those had been hard to stomach.

Frustrated by not knowing and feeling useless with the lack of answers, he pushed away from the computer and hightailed it out of the den.

"Marty?" his mom called out as he dashed past the kitchen. "Where's the fire?"

She followed him into the mudroom, where he shoved his feet into his boots.

"Going to Modesto, Ma." He snatched his hat off a hook and plopped it on his head, then reached for his jacket.

"Now?" She stepped into the small room; a frown creased her forehead while worry lit her eyes. "But it's almost dinner time."

"I know. I'm sorry." He leaned down and kissed her on the cheek. "I gotta go. I've got to see if he's there."

He patted his pockets one last time, making sure he had his phone, wallet, and keys.

"I'll call." He gave her a quick, reassuring smile, then bolted out the door.

Four and half hours later, he was sitting in his truck in front of a darkened rustic rancher with his heart sinking into the pit of his stomach. Tripp's motor coach was parked behind the house near a small barn, but the big blue Ford pickup was absent.

The man had to come home some time, so Marty pulled his collar up tighter, leaned back in the leather seat, and settled in for the wait. But as the hours ticked down and the stars inched across the black canvas of night, slowly giving way to the warm tones of a rising sun, a devastating realization began to crawl over his skin.

"Your hero ran off with another man even prettier."

"No." He sat up straight.

The air in the cab of the truck thinned, and he fought to breathe. The space closed in, pressed down on his chest, and he had to get out. He opened the door and spilled onto the gravel driveway. His legs had cramped from sitting all night, and he wobbled, grabbing onto the driver's side mirror for support. He sucked in large gulps of cool morning air and tried to rationalize, but his thoughts kept sliding back to Scott's words.

"He's gone and he ain't never coming back."

He shook his head. *No. Not true.*

That would mean their whole relationship, such as it was, had been a lie. That would mean Tripp had kept them in the closet not because he was afraid of coming out, but because he didn't really want to be out with *him*. That Marty had been nothing more than a convenient fuck while they were on the road. He knew that couldn't be true. Even though Tripp had never once said the words, he knew Tripp loved him and wanted him. He'd *felt* it.

"Your hero ran off with another man even prettier."

Or maybe Scott was right, and Marty had just projected what he'd wanted to believe.

"No!" He yelled at the empty house. "I heard your voice on the phone. I heard what you didn't say."

It wasn't a lie. Which meant Tripp's disappearance could only mean one thing, and he couldn't bear to let the thought take hold for fear it would manifest into reality.

He slammed his palm against the hood. "Fuck, Tripp! Where are you?"

Chapter Fourteen

Lily rushed out of the house and ran toward Marty's truck before he had come to a full stop.

"Thank God you're home." There was a sharp note of panic in her voice. She grabbed ahold of the door as he opened it to step down. "The guys have been calling for you every half hour."

"Why doesn't anyone call me on my fucking cell phone?" He yanked it out of his jacket pocket and scowled. The damn battery was dead again.

She grabbed him by the arm and hauled him toward the house.

"They found Tripp."

Relief barreled into him like a Brahma bull on a mission, and if Lily hadn't already been holding on to him, he'd have hit the ground. She wrapped an arm around his waist, and together they staggered into the house.

"Thank God." His voice was gruff from lack of sleep and the wear of too many emotions. "Where is he? Is he okay? What happened?"

Lily shook her head. "All I know is that he's in a hospital near Industry."

"But I called all the hospitals down there!"

"Don't yell at your sister." Buck shook a finger at him from where he sat at the kitchen table with his mom. "None of us know any details yet."

"I'm sorry. I'm just..."

"I know, son," Buck said.

His mom came around the table and hugged him tight, then reached around him for the phone.

"Here." She held it toward him. "Call and find out what's going on. Then I want you to sleep for a while before you go running off half-cocked again."

"I can't sleep right now." He dragged a hand over his face and grabbed the phone.

"You can't hardly stand up straight right now either. So sit."

He did.

His mom helped him out of his jacket and went to the counter to pour a hot cup of tea for him while he dialed.

"How is he?" Marty said before Kent had finished saying hello.

He heard a long exhale on the other end. "He's at the Arrowhead Regional Medical Center in Colton."

"How is he?"

"I don't know. The hospital won't tell anyone who isn't an immediate family member."

"But he's alive. He's going to be okay." Marty slumped down into his chair. His throat constricted, and his eyes began to sting. He could hear Kent's voice on the line, but he wasn't paying attention. Tripp was going to be okay. Nothing else mattered.

Finally, Kent's words filtered through the thick haze of relief. "Wait. Back up."

Kent spoke slower. "Eric, man. He sent Tripp's photo to all the ER departments with his phone number and told them to call him on the off chance Tripp had come in without identification. Here, hang on."

There was rustling in the background, and then a voice with an unmistakable accent spoke into the phone.

"Marty, it's Eric."

"Thank you so much."

"Anytime. Listen, being in the medical field, I was able to get some information. Tripp was admitted last week—late Sunday night. He'd been badly beaten, had no wallet or ID on him. They had to induce a coma shortly after he arrived, but I don't have deets on that. Apparently someone dropped him off at the entrance to the ER, but whoever it was didn't stick around to answer questions. They tell me he's stable now, which is good, but they didn't give me a time frame for when they'll wake him up."

"Jesus." Marty couldn't put voice to any of the thoughts bouncing around in his head. Just knowing that Tripp had been down there all this time, hurt and alone, no one knowing who he was or who to contact, made his heart ache. He had to get down there, be at Tripp's side when he woke up.

"Try not to worry," The hard edges of Eric's accent softened. "Being in an induced coma is probably the best thing to help him heal faster."

A stilted sob scraped up Marty's throat. *Induced coma*. God, what had they done to Tripp? When he found out who'd done this to his cowboy, there would be hell to pay. With interest.

And he had an idea just where to start.

"Thanks again for finding him." Resolve steadied his voice. "I gotta go now."

"Are you heading down to the hospital?"

"Yes. Right after I take care of something."

The line fell quiet for a moment. Eric lowered his voice, but the sharp edge was back. "Marty, whatever you're thinking of doing, don't. Go be there for Tripp, and take care of him. Everything else will work out as it should."

"Thanks, Eric. Thank the guys for me too." He hung up before Eric could say anything else Marty didn't want to hear, and dropped the phone to the table.

When he made to get up, small but deceptively strong hands pressed down on his shoulders.

"You aren't going anywhere until you've slept first," his mom said close to his ear.

"I'll strap you to your bed myself if you don't listen." His dad's voice was firm.

Marty made a point of eyeing the full cast on his dad's arm. Buck made his own point by raising a brow.

"Fine." Marty attempted to purse his lips, but a yawn forced its way out. Fatigue latched on, tugging hard at his consciousness. "Maybe just a couple hours of shut-eye."

Marty didn't remember making his way from the kitchen to his bedroom, and was dead to the world before his head hit the pillow.

By the time he awoke, tall shadows had fallen across his bedroom floor, indicating he'd clearly slept much longer.

He jumped out of bed, dug a small duffel bag out of the closet, and threw a few changes of clothing in it. He pulled on a pair of clean jeans and started to slip into a light green and tan shirt, but paused. Tripp had mentioned it was one of his favorites on Marty, liked the way it made his eyes brighter.

Marty took the shirt off, carefully folded it, and placed it in the duffel bag. He didn't want to risk getting that one dirty or torn, and would change into it when he got to the hospital. He grabbed a well-worn shirt and put it on.

Belt, watch, wallet, cell phone, he reached for the bag and stopped short when he noticed his phone charger on the night table. He tossed it into the bag and headed downstairs. The house was quiet, the kind of quiet that told Marty he was the only one home. He wandered into the kitchen and found a note stuck to the fridge with a cowboy-boot-shaped magnet. His parents had gone into town to see his dad's doctor, and Lily had gone with them. Breakfast was in the fridge. Marty wasn't hungry though. He had a lot of road to cover and a stop to make along the way that already had his stomach too knotted up to even think about food.

He flipped the note over to leave one of his own, and with a last minute check that he had everything, hitched his bag over his shoulder and headed out.

Four hours later, Marty turned off his truck and looked around. The house just outside of Stockton was a modest log rancher set back on what appeared to be a fair-sized spread. A large, black Dodge 3500 with a raised suspension was parked beside the matching log barn, which stood a few hundred yards south of the house. Off to the far side of the barn was a large paddock, where a few horses dozed in the late afternoon heat, their tails swishing lazily.

Movement caught Marty's eye, and he spotted Scott walking across the yard. The man's shoulders were rolled forward, his stride seemed a little slow and unsteady, and he appeared . . . smaller somehow. It didn't seem that Scott had noticed he had company yet, and when he disappeared inside the barn, Marty followed.

Scott sat on a bench, picked up a rag and poured Neatsfoot oil on it, then sifted through a pile of belts, leads, and reins.

Marty leaned against the doorframe. "I found Tripp."

Scott jerked to his feet and dropped the strip of leather he'd started to oil. Scott's gaze shot up to meet his, and for a second, Marty saw something he never imagined he'd see in Scott Gillard's eyes. Fear. Then his expression hardened, and the Scott he knew stood before him.

"Great. Now get the fuck off my property."

He would, but not until he had what he'd come for. "Yeah. Someone dropped him off at the ER in Industry after the rodeo. Seems he'd been roughed up pretty good and is in a coma."

Scott bent down to pick up his fallen bull belt and brushed dirt off it, then sat back down and resumed his task like he didn't have a care in the world. But the set of his shoulders and his shallow breathing told Marty otherwise.

"Got what he deserved then." Scott's voice was completely devoid of emotion.

"I'm thinking you know something about what happened that night." Marty pushed away from the doorframe and took a step forward. "And I'm thinking you need to te—"

The wind whooshed from his lungs and rough wood dug into his back. Scott had him pinned to the wall, hands around his throat dangerously close to cutting off his air.

"You don't know what the fuck you're talking about." Scott spat the words, and Marty saw then how sallow Scott's complexion was, how sunken and flat his red-rimmed eyes were, like the man hadn't slept in a week.

The week since Tripp had come out.

"It was you." Marty growled. Fury rose from depths he didn't know he even possessed. Intense, scalding, demanding penance. Something must have shown in his eyes because Scott's widened. Marty used the full force of his size to shove the man back and spin him around. He pinned Scott face-first against the wall with one arm pulled hard behind his back.

"Why did you do it?" He shoved Scott into the raw wood.

Scott struggled but couldn't break Marty's hold. "Get your fucking hands off me."

"Why did you do it?"

"I didn't—"

"You did!" Another shove. "He's in a fucking coma. Beat to shit. He didn't fucking deserve that."

"He did!" Scott shouted back with so much force and venom Marty felt the words like a blow to the jaw. "He deserved all of it and more! He was supposed to be my friend, but he's a fucking fag. Fucking you! They were supposed to fix it but they didn't. It's still there, and it's all Tripp's fucking fault."

"What the fuck are you talking about?"

"They didn't fucking cure me!"

". . . he had a cure."

The words echoed in Marty's mind, and he gasped as the realization hit him square in the chest.

Oh my God.

He leaned in close. "Are you gay, Scott?"

"*No!*" Scott's roar shook the walls around them and startled pigeons from their roost in the loft. Loose hay drifted to the barn floor in their wake. When the dust settled, all that remained was the sandpaper sound of Scott's harsh, rapid breaths.

"Jesus Christ." The pieces tumbled into place, and everything made sense now.

Scott's body went slack, and a weak sob seemed to claw its way painfully out of his chest.

"I don't want this." Scott's voice was thin and tired, like someone who'd well and truly given up. Face still pressed against the wall, even though Marty was no longer forcing him. He closed his eyes. "It's wrong. I want it to go away. The center was supposed to fix it, but they didn't. I'm still broken."

"Yes, Scott." Marty sighed. "You are broken, but not in the way that you think."

Still holding Scott in place with his hand behind his back, though the man made no more effort to fight back, Marty reached for his phone and punched in 9-1-1.

Chapter Fifteen

"So you're the mysterious Marty," the nurse sitting behind the counter said when he inquired about Tripp the next morning. Visiting hours had long since ended by the time he'd made it to the Arrowhead Medical Center the previous night. Not knowing how long he'd be there before Tripp woke up, he'd booked a room at the closest motel, intending to stay for as long as it took. Before he'd left his room that morning, he'd called his parents and friends with an update on what had happened with Scott.

After his blow-up and consequent breakdown, Scott hadn't said another word, other than to acknowledge that he understood his rights. The parting look he'd given Marty when he'd bent to climb into the backseat of the police cruiser, hands cuffed awkwardly behind his back, had been a blatant cry for help. But Scott Gillard was beyond his help.

"Pardon me, ma'am?"

"Our cowboy in there." The nurse tipped her head toward the hall. "When they brought him in he kept saying 'Marty' over and over. At first we thought that was his name, but then it was clear it wasn't, so we all started guessing who this Marty might be."

As good as it felt to know that Tripp had been calling out for him, it also broke his heart that he hadn't been there and Tripp's calls had gone unanswered.

"You don't look like a brother, and you're definitely not his son."

Marty didn't want to talk; he just wanted to know which room was Tripp's so he could get in there and be at his side when he woke. He also didn't want to be rude to the friendly nurse with the bright gray eyes and expectant expression. Sarah, her nametag read. He nodded. "You'd be right about that. So what is your guess now?"

She leaned forward, and her voice lowered to a conspiratorial tone. "I'm thinking boyfriend." She gave a quick nod and sat back, her eyes steady on his, but she played with the cap of a pen in her hand, opening, closing, opening, closing.

Marty shoved his hands into his pockets. "And why would you think that?"

She worried at her lip for a second. "You get to know how people are connected by the way they react in a crisis. And the way they say names. That man was calling for someone he loved with his whole heart."

Someone he loved with his whole heart.

Marty smiled, and a tightness he hadn't realized he'd been holding eased, leaving him feeling like he could finally take a full breath of air for the first time in a week.

"You'd be right. That's my man in there, and I'd really like to go to him now if I could."

"Oh! I'm so sorry." She jumped from her chair and came around from behind the desk. "I'm just so happy you're here now. He should have someone here who loves him. Right this way."

He followed her into a room three doors down from the nurse's station, and when his gaze landed on the broken, small-looking man in the bed, he gasped and stumbled into Sarah's back.

She turned to him and took a firm hold of his arm at the elbow to steady him. Concern sharpened her features and made her look younger.

"It looks worse than it is," she said. "I promise. All his vitals are strong, and his injuries are healing nicely. I'm sure they'll bring him out of the coma soon."

Marty nodded and tried a smile to reassure her, but he doubted it did much.

"Can I get you anything, hon?"

"No," he whispered. "I'm just going to sit with him."

She nodded and released his arm. "You give a shout if you change your mind. I'm here until the six o'clock shift change."

She turned and left him alone with Tripp, but Marty stayed where he stood in order to process what he was seeing.

Hoses and wires connected to Tripp at just about every possible point. Three ran into his left arm, a couple more on his temple, that nasty one up the nose, a catheter . . . A cast immobilized his entire leg, which was set in an elevated sling. Fading bruises mottled his face, a bandage stretched across the bridge of his nose—looked like it had been broken again—and there were stitches across his right temple and a butterfly bandage on his lower lip. The bedsheet was pulled midway up his torso, and one of those god-awful hospital gowns covered the rest, effectively hiding any further damage from view. Bandages covered both of Tripp's hands, leading him to believe Tripp had done some damage of his own to the attackers. Bruises covered his forearms, likely defensive wounds, and from the shape and number of them it looked like boot heels had been involved.

Helplessness at not having been able to prevent what had happened, at not having been there to help, burned the base of Marty's throat.

With nowhere to focus the growing anger for what had been done to Tripp, he shifted focus and scanned the room. It wasn't private, but the second bed was empty. The beds were set on opposite sides of the room, each with a table beside them and a single chair between the tables. He stepped deeper into the room, grabbed the chair and dragged it across the polished linoleum to the side of Tripp's bed.

He sat, took his hat off and set it on the table, and then really studied Tripp. He wanted to reach out, hold his hand, pull him into his arms, but he had no idea just how much internal damage had been done or what else might be broken. But Tripp's slow and steady breathing was a comforting balm.

"Tripp." His throat tightened, making the word crack, and his vision blurred. He leaned forward and brushed his fingertip over the temple free of stitches and into jet-black hair that already needed a trim. "I love you. I'm here, and I'm not going anywhere until you come back to me. You hear me? I'm staying right here."

Soft rustling pushed at the edges of his awareness again, along with a pleasantly sweet smell. Not a perfume exactly, or even flowers, but something . . . feminine. Familiar, but he couldn't place from where or why.

Light seemed to come from one direction, disappearing into the darkness at the contours of his eyelids. The sense of not being alone overcame him again. Fuzzy shapes blotted out the dim light; the smell increased and faded. A steady, distant beep grew progressively louder until it sounded too close to his head, and the surface of his skin began to tingle. He tried to swallow, but his throat felt unused and hurt. More sounds seeped into his mind, creating a disjointed mental picture show. Door opening and closing, candles burning, footsteps, pressure and darkness closing around him, and then brightly colored flowers growing from between his toes.

"No," he said, his voice gruff. That wasn't right. He heard an intake of . . . breath? He frowned. He wasn't alone, but he didn't know who was with him or where he was, and his eyelids refused to lift so he could see for himself.

"Tripp?" a female voice whispered. "Tripp, can you hear me?"

Yes. The voice in his head was strong, but he couldn't tell if he'd actually spoken aloud. Maybe? He nodded his head once.

Weight settled lightly on his shoulder. The voice said, "I'll be right back."

Sure thing.

Retreating footsteps. Distant voices. The steady *beep, beep, beep* . . . Hospital. Certain that's where he was, but unsure as to why.

There was a rustling sound to his left and a soft snuffle, like a snore. Someone else was in the room. He willed his eyes to open, and this time his lids lifted a sliver, but he couldn't make anything out. Just blurry shapes and colors, nothing defined.

Two forms entered the room and came to a halt at his side. His vision cleared a little, and he managed to make out a man in a long white coat and woman in powder blue scrubs.

"Mr. Colby?"

A short laugh tumbled from Tripp's mouth. No one called him "mister." Ever.

"Mr. Colby." The doctor moved to the end of the bed. "Do you know where you are?"

Tripp nodded. "Hospital."

Something poked the bottom of his foot, and he jerked.

"Good. I'm Dr. Anders at the Arrowhead Center in Colton. Do you know why you're here?"

Tripp shook his head. What the hell was he doing in Colton? The last thing he remembered was...

"Marty?" Panic shot through his chest, and he tried to sit up, but a flash fire in his guts pushed him back down. Pain. Everywhere. Head, neck, ribs... his whole body screamed abuse.

"Easy." The nurse's soothing voice, along with the sweet scent he remembered, calmed him. "He's fine. Asleep on the other bed."

Tripp rolled his head slowly to the side. He couldn't make out Marty's features, but he could see his shape. God, all he wanted to do was go over there, crawl into the bed, and curl up beside him. Assure himself Marty was okay. He didn't know why, but something... No. Someone had threatened Marty. Maybe. The noise in his head made it hard to be sure.

"Okay, then." Dr. Anders made a notation on his chart. "Everything looks good here. I'll be back to check on you again in a few hours. Just press the button by your right hand if you need anything."

Tripp nodded but didn't pull his attention away from Marty. His eyelids drooped. Everything was okay now, though. Marty was all he needed.

When he opened his eyes again, daylight was filtering through the window into the room, and his vision cleared faster. He turned to the other bed, but it was empty. He frowned. Had he dreamed seeing Marty the night before? He wasn't even sure that it *had* been the night before.

"Don't worry, hon." A woman's voice drew his attention to the doorway. "I made him go downstairs for something to eat. I don't think that boy's eaten more than a granola bar since he's been here."

"How long?" Tripp's voice sounded rusty as it scratched over his vocal chords.

She stepped up beside him and took his wrist in her hand, pressing her fingers against the underside while she focused on her watch.

"You've been here for eleven days sleeping it off." She released his wrist and winked at him before gently sticking a thermometer in his ear. "Your boyfriend has been here for three days. I couldn't get him to leave, and we didn't need the other bed, so I did a little sweet talking with the higher-ups to let him sleep there."

She pulled the thermometer from his ear, checked the reading, and walked over to the foot of the bed to make her notations on his chart.

"Can you tell me what happened?"

Dr. Anders entered the room before she could answer. She smiled warmly, nodded at the doctor, and snuck out behind him.

Anders picked up the chart. "How are you feeling?"

"Ready for the World Championships."

The doctor leveled a long, serious look at him, and Tripp could see the wheels turning in the doctor's head. How to break the bad news... With a sinking feeling in his stomach, he braced himself.

"You've suffered extensive injuries, Mr. Colby." Dr. Anders replaced the chart and walked over to Tripp's side. "Most you'll recover from completely: concussion, broken nose, several deep lacerations requiring stitches, three broken and two cracked ribs. But your left leg didn't fare quite as well. The femur and tibia were broken in several places, requiring steel rods and pins. The kneecap was shattered and tendons ruptured."

Tripp's stomach bottomed out while he tried to put the injury list into some sort of perspective he could understand.

"You'll need considerable physical therapy. You'll likely have permanent restriction of movement, especially when fully extending your leg, and it's doubtful you'll ever walk without a cane. But the good news is you *will* walk again and live out a normal productive life."

Never walk without a cane...?

His guts flipped, and a crawling sensation tightened his skin. He shook his head. No. Not good enough.

"Unfortunately, you won't be able to ride or compete again. Especially at the professional level." Anders placed a hand on his biceps. "I'm sorry, Mr. Colby. I'm afraid your rodeoing days are over."

He opened his mouth to argue, but the words his lips formed remained silent. White noise assaulted his eardrums, drowning out whatever else the good doctor was saying, while blood pulsed through his veins with enough force to split them open.

No. Not true. He was a bull rider. A world fucking *champion*. Champions got back up, dusted themselves off, slapped on a Band-Aid, and hopped right back in the saddle. Just like he would, as soon as he got out of this fucking hospital. Anders and his dire prediction could fuck right off.

You know it's true.

The back of his throat constricted and burned. He couldn't accept that. Wouldn't. Rodeo was all he had, all he knew.

He squeezed his eyes shut, and when he opened them again, the room was empty.

Realization struck him harder than any bull ever had. His life was as empty as the room he lay in. He'd had rodeo and he'd had Marty, but without either, what was there now? Who was he?

"Your rodeoing days are over."

Tripp furrowed his brows, and numbing cold seeped into his flesh, his bones. *What am I without rodeo?*

Nothing.

No career, no identity, no purpose—just an empty broken shell.

Oh, but he was out now. He pursed his lips at the thought. Maybe Marty would take him back, but why? How could he be a part of Marty's life if he couldn't even ride? Unless he wanted to follow Marty around on the circuit like some fucking buckle bunny. Or hand out event programs, if he could manage that while leaning on a damn cane.

"Your rodeoing days are over." Around and around went the doctor's verdict in his head.

He was done.

Thirty-three years old and his career was over.

His life was over.

Relief nearly toppled Marty to his knees when he returned to the room and found Tripp staring at the ceiling. He couldn't get to Tripp's bedside fast enough, but he did manage not to sprint the short distance. Tripp was awake, finally, and everything would be right with the world now. A smile overtook his face, so big it threatened to give him cheek cramps.

"Hey," Marty said, his voice soft, and gently placed a hand on Tripp's upper arm. He needed to touch, to feel warm skin, assure himself Tripp was going to be okay.

Pale blue eyes shifted to meet his; a sparkle of warmth flickered over their surface, and then discolored lids dropped to block them from view. Tension coursed from Tripp in measured waves, and his mouth pressed into a firm line.

"Marty..." Reedy, raw, but it was the note of grief in Tripp's deep voice that made Marty's heart ache for what Tripp had gone through, how much pain he must be in. If only he could somehow take it all away, make it so Tripp would never feel anything but happiness and peace.

"Do you need me to get the doctor back in here? More pain meds?"

Tripp opened his eyes. Need and hope, despair and anger, chased each other in erratic circles in their depths, until one slow blink erased all trace of emotion. Staring back at him now was the old blank mask Tripp had always hidden behind, times a thousand. Unease tickled at his consciousness.

"Doc says I'll never walk normal again." Tripp's voice matched his expression: cold, flat, and just a little scary. He turned away from Marty, gaze locking on the ceiling again. "Says for sure my riding days are over."

Oh, my God. Marty's heart gave a nauseating lurch in his chest. "He doesn't know what he's talking about. Doesn't know you."

Tripp shook his head. "My spurs done been hung. No more rodeo for this cowboy."

"No." Marty leaned forward and put a hand over Tripp's, letting him know he was there and would always be there, but Tripp didn't return the grip. "You'll rodeo again. You just need some time to heal and th—"

"Stop." Tripp squeezed his eyes shut. "Just. Stop."

Marty studied Tripp, watched a muscle twitch in his jaw, but couldn't find any cracks in the wall he'd thrown up. "You can't give up. You can't let this change anything, or they win."

Tripp yanked his hand out from under Marty's and shot a glare at him so icy that his lungs froze mid-inhale. "*They* wouldn't have won or lost anything if I hadn't come out."

Marty sucked in a sharp breath. "You can't mean that."

"If I'd stayed where I was, I wouldn't be here right now. I'd still be able to ride." Tripp narrowed his eyes, but a flash of vulnerability danced behind their glacial surface and tugged at Marty. "I'd still be someone."

"You *are* someone, Tripp."

Tripp huffed, the sound weak but obstinate. "No. That's where you're wrong. I'm nothing without rodeo."

"That's not true, and you know it."

"Do I?" The edge in Tripp's voice cut a ragged swath through Marty's heart. "You've always had family and friends who've stood by you your whole life. Me? I had rodeo. That's it."

"You have me."

"No, I don't!" Tripp's voice cracked like a whip, and Marty jerked back as though he'd been struck by it. "You dumped me because I wouldn't come out, remember? You wanted me to face my fucking demons. Well I did, and look what it got me." Tripp motioned toward his leg, and Marty shivered, his mouth going dry. *No.* He shook his head. *Not true.* "Didn't you hear me when I said that I can't ride or compete again? Ever?"

"I don't care about that." Even as his body shook and his flesh crawled, Marty kept his voice strong enough to hide the panic scratching at his mind, darkening the edges of his vision. He could not, would not, let Tripp believe he was any less than he had been before. "You're the same Tripp Colby I fell in love with, and whether or not you can compete changes nothing. Rodeo isn't who you are."

"It's *all* I was!" Tripp punched the mattress by his thigh and hissed, his complexion turning ashen. His voice was tight and strained when he continued, but no less cutting. "Now it's all gone and I have nothing. I *am* nothing. And looking at you only reminds me of that."

Surprise and regret flashed in Tripp's widened eyes, and a fault line trembled through his hard façade. The only signs that he realized what he'd said, but the cracks sealed back up before it could take hold. The poison in those harsh words had already been released into the air, spreading like a deadly virus.

"Are—" Marty choked. His voice caught in a stranglehold. "Are you saying this is my fault?"

"I'm saying my rodeo days are over." Tripp returned his stare to the ceiling, that hard cold voice driving another nail into Marty's chest. "And so are we."

"Tripp—"

"Just leave."

Marty opened his mouth, but no words formed, no sound came out. His entire body froze, except for the rapid pulse of blood pumping ice through the big vein in his neck.

Tripp turned blazing eyes on him, his lips peeled back. "Did you hear me? Get the fuck out!"

Marty jumped, staggered backward, and bumped into the chair behind him. Its legs screeched as it bounced across the floor, the sound barely reaching his ears. He swayed for a second, head spinning and stomach crawling up his throat, certain he was going to collapse.

So this is what the world falling out from under you feels like.

If he'd just been happy with the way things were, Tripp would be fine, *they'd* be fine.

Somewhere in the back of his mind, he knew that wasn't true, but the little voice of reason couldn't claw its way through the heavy cloak of guilt squeezing around him like a vise.

"I'm sorry, Tripp." The words broke, scraping over tight vocal chords. He raked a hand through the air, looking for something to grab onto, reaching for Tripp. He didn't know which, only that the tether keeping him grounded had snapped and a chasm had opened between them, widening at lightning speed. "I didn't mean to. I just wanted . . ." His breath hitched, his voice ragged and hoarse. "Forgive me. Please. I'm so sorry."

What more could he say or do, except what he'd been so adamantly told to: leave. He turned and bolted out the door, his steps jerky and uncoordinated. He thought maybe he heard Tripp call his name, but knew it was only wishful thinking. Tripp had made it more than clear that they were through, and he was right. Because Marty *had* wanted him to come out, and in doing so, Tripp had lost everything.

And now, so had he.

Chapter Sixteen

"JesusFuckingChrist!"

Marty jumped so high off the bed he damn near hit his head on the ceiling. His heart shot into his throat, and his skin pulled so tight over his bones he felt like it would rip open and spill all his insides out onto the floor.

His mind raced. What were Kent, Bridge, and Eric doing in his bedroom, and why the hell was he wet and standing in a puddle of ice-cold water in the middle of his bed? Water trickled down his bare chest, and he kicked at an ice cube beside his foot when he noticed a bucket in Bridge's hand.

"What the fuck?" He glared at his friends and stepped down to drier ground. He snatched a shirt from the piles of clothes scattered all over his floor and wiped his chest. "That felt like a fucking cattle prod, you assholes. Could have given me a fucking heart attack!"

"Martin Anderson Fairgrave! Mind your language in my house!" His mom's voice carried up from downstairs.

"Argh!" Marty doubled over when the cold water seeped into his boxers, and his dick recoiled in terror. He yanked them off and, unmindful of his audience, rooted buck naked through the flannel-topped denim mountains that buried the carpet.

Eric whistled. "Nice ass."

Somebody snorted. Marty found a dry pair of jeans and pulled them on.

"That's disgusting." Kent scrunched up his nose. "When was the last time you did your laundry?"

He buttoned up the fly. "Until it walks on its own, it's good to go."

His friends shared a glance.

"Seriously." Marty shivered and navigated his way across the room to his dresser drawers, where he dug out a warm sweater. One that was actually clean. "What are you guys doing here, and why couldn't you wake me up like a normal person?"

Kent harrumphed. "Normal people don't sleep until past three o'clock."

"This is an intervention," Bridge said.

Marty's eyebrows shot up, and he looked at each of them, waiting for the punch line, but no. Their matching expressions said "I'm totally dead serious." Marty groaned and rubbed his hands over his face. He needed a shave, probably a shower, and to brush his teeth. But fuck it. Wasn't like anyone gave a shit how he looked.

"I don't need an intervention. I need a beer."

"Exactly what I just said." Bridge crossed his arms.

Marty ducked his head and walked toward the doorway. He had to get away from his friends before they made him think about things he didn't want to think about, but the three of them formed a solid wall.

"Move."

"Not happening."

Marty crossed his arms and stared hard out the window. This was their party. He had nothing to say.

"We've had enough," Bridge said. "You've been sulking and pouting and drinking yourself into oblivion for the better part of two months now."

"No, I haven't." He knew it was a lie the second it left his mouth, but the guys didn't call him out for it.

"I saw Tripp."

Marty jerked and sucked in a breath, but he bit back taking the bait. He refused to engage in this little *intervention*. He refused to ask how Tripp was doing, even though the words burned a hole in the back of his throat as they clamored for escape.

"He looks like shit too," Eric said. "Just like you."

Marty turned to look at Eric, who nodded. That wasn't what Marty had expected to hear. Tripp had kicked him out of his life.

He had made the choice, and as far as Marty knew, had crawled happily back into his closet. As much as he could after publicly coming out, but he guessed if Tripp stayed away from the rodeo world, he could retreat into anonymity.

"You need to go see him," Kent said.

Marty shook his head. "I can't."

"Why not?"

"Because he threw me out of his life, that's why!" Didn't they get it? He'd already told them what had happened that day at the hospital. The day the rug had been ripped out from under his feet and his world had crashed down around him.

"I told you this. I pushed him too hard because I didn't want a closeted boyfriend. I was selfish. Wanted what I wanted and to hell with anyone else. He hates me now." Marty dropped his hands to his sides and looked at the floor. The toe of a sock peeking out from under a pair of jeans drew his attention.

"Because of me he lost everything. Because of me his life is ruined." His voice sounded distant, the words bitter-tasting. Logically, somewhere in the back of his mind he knew he wasn't the one who'd ended Tripp's career, but he *had* played a part in what led to it. He had to live with that. And Tripp had made his feelings painfully clear. "He doesn't want me anywhere near him. So, no. I will not be going to see him."

Kent shook his head. "You're fixated on what Tripp was throwing out in the wake of bad news, not what he really meant."

Marty snapped his eyes up, glaring at Kent. "How the hell would you know what he meant? You weren't there."

"Didn't have to be." Kent turned to Eric and nodded.

Eric hooked his thumbs through his belt loops. "I was covering a shift for a coworker, and we had a stop at the medical center in Modesto. They have a physio department, and Tripp was there. He approached me. After a few minutes of shooting the shit about nothing, he asked me how you were doing, hoped you were okay, and then said he hoped I was treating you right. If I wasn't then he promised me he'd track me down and string me up by parts I'd rather not think about hanging by."

Bridge made a funny sound and took a step closer to Eric. The move was almost... territorial. Marty cocked his head.

"What's going on here?" He looked between Eric and Bridge. Kent cleared his throat.

"What's going on here"—Eric took a step forward, his accent somehow softer—"is that those weren't the questions or concerns of a man who didn't give a shit."

Marty wanted to believe that was true, but it didn't match up with the man who'd thrown him out of his life two months ago. A tiny kernel of hope tried to crack its shell, but Marty refused to help it open. He couldn't bear Tripp rejecting him again, and definitely didn't want Tripp to come to resent him for representing what he no longer had.

"You didn't hear the things he said to me." Marty turned to face the window and frowned, afraid to believe but desperately wanting to. "You didn't hear his voice."

"And you listened *only* to those words." Kent's hand landed on his shoulder and squeezed briefly. "End your pity party here, and think on it, Smarts. You'll hear it differently."

One by one his friends hugged him and then silently left him alone with his thoughts. He sat heavily on a dry spot on the edge the bed while his emotions battled: guilt, hope, doubt... around and around they went. Could it be true that Tripp still cared? That he'd only been railing in anger after learning the extent of his injuries?

Instead of storming out of the house and heading for the bar in town, which was what he'd fully intended to do, he gathered his clothes from the floor and threw them into the wash. Then he stripped down and took a long, thorough shower.

He replayed that horrible, last conversation with Tripp while hot water sluiced over his skin. One by one, the words began to tumble into place. Tripp's entire world had been wrapped up in bull riding, and when that had been ripped away, so had his sense of identity. In his worked-up state, he'd managed to convince himself he wasn't good enough anymore for himself or for Marty, and that his life was over. And when Marty had argued, Tripp had dug deeper into the sludge and slung words guaranteed to leave a mark. And they had for far too many weeks. But now that Marty looked at them closer, rolled them around in his mind, the forces behind the words became crystal clear: fear, pain, and rage. Tripp had come out of a coma only hours before, was doped up on narcotics, and had just received life-altering news from the doctor. It made sense that he'd needed to lash out, and Marty had been the first person standing there to take the brunt of it.

A small smile tipped the edges of Marty's mouth. The clouds parted to let the sun shine through and the oppressive weight of guilt lifted from his shoulders, leaving hope in its wake. For the first time since that day, he could finally see clearly.

And now he had a cowboy to see about.

"Kudos, boys." Marty saluted to his friends *in absentia*.

He jumped out of the shower, shaved, dressed in a favorite shirt of Tripp's, packed a small bag, and headed downstairs.

"Now there's my boy," his mom said when he entered the kitchen. He poured a glass of iced tea and handed it to her, then poured another for himself. He smiled, and they clinked glasses in an unspoken toast. She stretched up and kissed his cheek. "I can't tell you how good it is to see you smile again."

"Ma." Marty rolled his eyes.

"Don't 'ma' me." She bumped her shoulder into his. "Where are you off to?"

He cleared his throat. "Going to pay a visit to Tripp."

She smiled. "Good."

A wave of déjà vu washed over Marty when he found himself once again sitting in the driveway of Tripp's Modesto rancher. Only this time warm light from inside the house spilled out into the night, and the big blue F-150 sat right next to where Marty had parked.

He glanced at the duffel bag on his passenger seat and debated whether or not he should take it with him. The confident side of him said of course, but that niggling little negative side argued against it. In the end, he made his way to the front door of the house empty-handed. Wasn't like he'd have far to go to come back and get it later.

He knocked on the front door, and when it swung open, he couldn't help the smile that spread across his face. Eric was right. Tripp didn't look like he'd been taking care of himself, but it was Tripp, and no matter what shape he was in, he was still gorgeous to Marty.

Tripp's eyes widened, but he recovered and blanked his expression. He'd slowed though. Whether he knew it or not, that stoic façade didn't snap into place like it used to. And damn good thing too. Marty didn't want to see it ever again.

"It's time to drop the act now, don't you think?" He muscled his way inside. The house looked the same as he remembered, decorated in warm earth tones with dark leather furniture and rustic accents; he'd always felt so comfortable here. He stepped into the sunken living room and turned around. Tripp was still standing in the entryway, both the door and his mouth wide open.

"Wh-what?"

"Might want to close the door." Marty inclined his head. "You're letting in all the 'skeeters."

Tripp pushed it closed, his gaze locked on Marty's. He limped across the foyer, relying heavily on a cane to keep his weight off his braced knee, but didn't step down into the living room.

"What are you doing here?"

"We've both been through enough now, I think."

Tripp bowed his head and stared at a spot on the floor.

"You really hurt me, Tripp." Marty paused when he noticed Tripp's already sagging shoulders slump further. He didn't want to see Tripp slide deeper into himself. He wanted to pull the man into his arms and comfort him, but they had some air to clear. "You were such an asshole, but I've figured it out, with a little help."

Tripp shifted on his cane, but still didn't raise his head or speak.

"Did you really think I wouldn't catch on? Granted, it took some creative assistance, but—"

"I don't know what you're talking about." Tripp's voice was low and reedy.

"I think you do." Marty took a step forward. "What you did, the way you pushed me away? Hate didn't do that. Love did."

Tripp shook his head, but it seemed halfhearted, and his chest rose and fell quicker.

"Yes." He took another step forward. "I finally figured out that you were hurting and lashing out. But also that you loved me enough to do what you thought was best for me. To make sure I moved on to find someone I better deserved, who could offer me more. No matter what the cost. But there's something you missed in that messed-up reasoning—which I'm laying all that blame on having just come out of a coma, by the way—and that's this: No one could ever offer me more because you already gave me your heart. It's mine, and you can't take it back. I plan on keeping it safe with me for always."

Tripp tilted his head, and a lock of black hair fell to obscure his eyes further, but Marty caught how he pursed his lips.

"I love you." Marty pushed everything he felt for this man into his voice, hoping Tripp would hear it, feel it, *believe* it. "I love *you*. I don't care if you never rodeo again. I don't care that you may never walk without a cane."

Marty took his hat off and stepped back up onto the foyer. "I care about this." He reached out and gently placed a hand over Tripp's heart, and Tripp leaned into the touch while his shoulders gave an almost imperceptible shake.

"I care about this." Marty moved his hand up to Tripp's head and ran his fingers across his temple, threading into his hair. He pushed the wayward strands from Tripp's eyes and saw they were closed, cheek damp, and his shoulders shook again.

"I care about this," Marty whispered and tenderly ran the pad of his thumb under Tripp's eye, brushing away the tear that had spilled free.

A sound that might have been a sob or maybe a gasp escaped from Tripp. He dropped his cane and threw his arms around

Marty. Marty's hat fell from his grip, and he pulled Tripp tighter to him.

"God, Marty." Tripp's voice sounded as shattered as the man in Marty's arms. "I love you so much."

Marty closed his eyes and buried his face in the crook of Tripp's neck. All the hope he'd been shoving down, trying so hard not to believe in, sprung free. Finally, the words he'd wanted to hear for so long, and they were the sweetest music to ever play over his eardrums.

"Tripp..."

"I was so angry and out of my head and—" Tripp's voice hitched and he sucked in a deep breath.

"Shhh." Marty moved his hand in circles over Tripp's back. "It's okay now."

"No. Christ. The things I said." Tripp tried to pull away, but Marty tightened his hold. No way was he letting go of this man again. But Tripp didn't put up a fight. "I didn't mean any of it. I didn't know how to take it back, and then it was too late."

"I know." Marty cupped the back of Tripp's head. "And it was never too late."

"I wanted better for you. You deserve better than me, someone who has it together, like Eric."

Marty smiled. "Having it together is relative. Eric doesn't hold a candle to you. No one does. And you will always be my champion, Tripp Colby. It was never about the buckle."

Tripp leaned back, and this time Marty let him. Their eyes met, and Tripp's bright blue gaze glittered with a sincerity that reflected in his voice. "Can you ever forgive me? Please? I promise I will spend the rest of my life making it up to you if you'll let me."

"Yes." Marty angled his head and kissed the column of Tripp's neck. "Yes." He cupped the side of Tripp's head and leaned in to claim his mouth in a desperate kiss. He had to taste Tripp, feel him, reacquaint their bodies, and Tripp kissed him back with equal hunger, as if he were trying to climb inside Marty. The thought sent a depth charge of heat exploding in Marty's belly.

"Start now. Take me to bed."

Tripp nodded and turned quickly. He took a step and sucked in a sharp breath, his complexion turning ashen.

Marty wrapped him in his arms. "I've got you, babe. Lean on me."

"This is . . . embarrassing." Tripp looked away and his shoulders slumped forward. "Fuck."

"This is nothing." Marty placed a lingering kiss to Tripp's temple. "And you have a promise to keep."

Tripp looked up into Marty's eyes with a mix of uncertainty and longing.

Marty smiled and nodded. He tucked Tripp against his side and walked them both down the hall toward the bedroom. He peppered Tripp with kisses to keep him from thinking about his leg, or how he wasn't good enough, or any other nonsense. Marty knew what was good for him, and he had his arms full of it right now.

They stumbled into the bedroom, and Marty turned Tripp to face him. He cupped Tripp's head with both hands and leaned in to continue the kiss he'd started in the entryway. Desperation to experience all of Tripp again buzzed just under the surface of his skin, clamoring for more, faster, harder, everything Tripp had to give, but he kept it in check. There was no need to rush, no need to charge headlong into release. They had time, all the time in the world, and Marty planned on savoring every single second of it. And savor he did, enjoying the feel of their tongues as they slid together, wrapped around each other, sensually lunging and retreating.

He angled his head to deepen the kiss, and Tripp opened further. Their teeth bumped, and Tripp's hands came up to tangle in Marty's hair, tugging gently. Marty let his head fall back at the unspoken request, even though he didn't want to break the kiss, and Tripp licked and sucked and nipped at his neck and jaw and chin.

"Ah, Tripp." He groaned and pulled away. Needing the feel of Tripp's mouth back on his, he resumed their impassioned kissing until the desire to feel more of his man became impossible to resist.

He tugged at Tripp's shirt and yanked it free of his jeans. Buttons were too much work just then, so he pulled it over Tripp's head and tossed it to the floor. Tripp looked up at him with those piercing eyes, so intense, so focused, and smiled slow and sexy. Marty's heart swelled so big inside his chest he thought it might pop right out.

"I love you so much," he whispered. "You have no idea."

"I think maybe I do." Tripp's voice was a ragged, smoky rasp that sent shivers chasing each other over Marty's skin—skin that cried out for Tripp to touch every inch of it.

Marty pressed Tripp backward onto the bed, gently enough not to jar his leg, but forcefully enough for him to know he meant business. Tripp smiled up at him, and his eyes flashed with a desire that Marty knew was reflected in his own.

Marty yanked his own shirt over his head and knelt on the bed. He crawled up to straddle Tripp and ran his hands slowly over the smooth, heated torso, his eyes following their exploration with rapt attention. Tripp was a little thinner, but no less beautiful.

"I love how you look at me." Tripp tangled a hand into Marty's hair.

Marty met his eyes and silently vowed that he would always look at Tripp that way, always make sure his cowboy knew just how much he loved him, just how perfect he was, exactly as he was. The words tangled up, so he leaned down to tell Tripp another way. He kissed a reverent, crooked path from neck to navel, making lazy stops along the way to pull a nipple into his mouth and gently bite, slide his tongue tenderly over the rise and fall of bones and circle Tripp's belly button. Tripp grunted and squirmed beneath him, and he knew Tripp understood.

Marty moved lower and traced the hard erection trapped behind denim with his mouth. Tripp rocked his hips up in a wordless plea for more. Marty made quick work of popping the button and pulling the zipper down, smiling at Tripp's loud, relieved sigh.

"Better?"

"Almost. Little more and it'll be perfect."

Marty chuckled. He rocked back on his heels and playfully smacked Tripp's hip. "Up."

Tripp lifted, and Marty started to tug the jeans and boxers from Tripp's body, but a sharp intake of breath made Marty pause. He looked up to see Tripp's eyes widened and a hint of panic in their clear depths.

Marty crawled up the bed and kissed Tripp with every last bit of his love and desire until the tension seeped from Tripp's body in complete surrender. He pulled back just enough to look into Tripp's eyes, their lips brushing as he spoke. "That is a part of you now, but it isn't all of you. It won't, it can't, change how I feel about you or how I see you."

Marty held his gaze, and when Tripp nodded, a shy smile breaking free, Marty shimmied back down and carefully removed the last of Tripp's clothing. He shot a reassuring glance at Tripp and looked down to follow the line of surgical trails that ran from hip to knee and knee to shin.

He sighed. "God, you're a beautiful man."

He bent down and placed a soft kiss at the lowermost end of the trail, and Tripp tensed. Marty dragged his lips up and left another invisible mark with his mouth. Again and again, following the path until Tripp's body became relaxed and pliable. Once he reached where the road ended near the juncture of Tripp's hip, he turned to a part of his cowboy he had missed worshipping for far too long.

Not wanting to waste another second, Marty started at the base of Tripp's cock and licked a wet path to the tip before swallowing him down as deep as he could take him. A burst of musk flooded his senses and made his mouth water.

Tripp jerked up, pushing deeper into his throat, and hands fisted in his hair. A ragged curse echoed around them before he heard Tripp say, "Perfect."

Marty smiled around the silky, hard flesh in his mouth and set to work creating a sensual slide and suck, up and down, capping with a swirl of his tongue and then back down. He cupped Tripp's balls with one hand, holding, squeezing, and rolling them on his fingers. He placed his other hand on Tripp's stomach, sliding it slowly upward until he reached Tripp's chin. Tripp opened his mouth and sucked Marty's fingers, and Marty's cock throbbed painfully within the constraints of his jeans.

Marty groaned, and with one more powerful suck, he released Tripp from his mouth and jumped up from the bed.

Tripp shot a disapproving glare at him. "Not perfect anymore."

Marty kicked out of his boots while unbuttoning his jeans. "Gotta get these off."

He sprang free with so much relief it sent a shudder through him.

"Yes," Tripp hissed. "Put your boots back on."

Marty raised an eyebrow, but the salacious grin and wicked glint Tripp bestowed on him had him jumping back into his boots without another thought.

Instead of picking up where he'd left off, Marty crawled up beside Tripp, half on, half off his body. He pulled at Tripp until they faced each other on their sides, pressed together, mouth to mouth, chest to chest, thigh to thigh, cock to cock. Everywhere their skin met sent an explosion of heat and electricity shooting through Marty's core.

"Make love to me, Tripp," he said between kisses. "Please."

Tripp reached between their bodies and grasped both their cocks in his hand. He tugged slow and sure, pace matching the sensual slide of their mouths and tongues as Marty deepened the kiss.

Tripp released them. "Roll over." His voice was a low rasp that sent a shiver of excitement through Marty. He flipped around, molding his backside against Tripp's front, and Tripp rocked forward, his cock sliding along the crack of Marty's ass. Marty moaned his desire and reached around to put his hand on Tripp's hip and draw him closer.

Tripp nuzzled against Marty's head, and hot, moist breath ghosted over the shell of his ear. "Get the lube."

Marty cracked an eye open and groaned. He was on the side of the bed closest to the nightstand, but far enough from it that reaching over would mean pulling away from Tripp. Even a second away from the man would be too much. But the lube ... He took a deep breath and lunged for the drawer, pawed inside until his hand landed on the bottle, and shot back into that glorious pocket of heat. He trembled from the brief separation, or maybe that was anticipation.

Tripp took the bottle from him and kissed his shoulder before leaning back. Marty heard the cap pop. Lips nipped at his skin, and cool fingers slid down through his crease, over his hole, and palmed his balls before retreating and repeating the motion, lingering longer and pressing deeper against his entrance with each pass.

A rush of sensations skated and bounced under and over the surface, making him want to crawl out of his skin. His body shook with an uncontrollable need that stole his breath.

He rocked back into Tripp. "Love me."

"I do." Tripp planted a soft kiss on his biceps. "More than I can say."

"Show me."

Tripp nudged Marty's leg up, and then he felt the press of Tripp's cockhead at his hole. He tilted his hips to open himself as much as possible and twisted so he could angle his head back. He didn't need to tell Tripp what he wanted. Tripp's lips met his, mouths opening and tongues dancing, just as Tripp pushed up and breached him. A deep guttural sound filled the air, and Marty broke the kiss to drop his head onto the pillow. He wasn't sure if that groan came from him or not, but the next one definitely did when Tripp rocked deeper into him. Inch by slow-burning inch, until his body relaxed around Tripp's cock, now fully seated inside of him. Good lord, it was the most glorious thing Marty had ever known. Tripp put his hand under Marty's thigh and pulled his leg up higher, and they settled into a steady, languid rhythm. Each stroke into his body felt like a caress, felt like love and hope and a future. All the things Marty wanted with Tripp, all the things he wanted to give to Tripp.

They moved as one, rocking and thrusting and grunting together until Marty felt the energy build around them, within Tripp, within himself. His orgasm rose with steady intensity and teetered on the edge of release. He reached down and took hold of himself, but Tripp's hand closed over his, and together he worked their hands up and down his shaft. He gasped. "So close."

"Yes." Tripp pumped into him harder, faster, until he pressed in deep and stayed there, his body shaking and Marty's name spilling from his mouth like a prayer. Marty's orgasm crashed through the gate and exploded so powerfully his vision flickered out and stars flashed in the aftershock.

They stayed that way, melded together in euphoric bliss while their racing hearts slowed to normal. Finally, Tripp eased himself from Marty's body, and Marty turned in his arms, sated beyond words, but he didn't need any now. He'd said everything he needed to, and Tripp had heard.

Marty tucked Tripp into him so his chin rested on top of Tripp's head, and he pulled the bedsheet up over their cooling bodies.

"Perfect," Tripp mumbled just before his breathing evened out.

Yes, Marty thought as sleep dragged him down.
Perfect.

Epilogue

"I have a plan!"

Marty lifted his eyelids to find Tripp lying on his side, looking down at him with dancing baby blues. He smiled and rolled into Tripp's warm body, nuzzling the strong jaw with his nose and nipping playfully at his neck.

In the months since Tripp had given up the misguided notion that Marty deserved better, he'd bloomed and become the man Marty knew had always been there. The one he'd only ever been able to catch rare, unguarded glimpses of. Every day Tripp grew more confident and carefree. He smiled more, laughed more, and walked right at Marty's side in public. He hadn't kissed Marty publicly yet, but he had held his hand and occasionally stuck a hand into the back pocket of his jeans. Open admiration and love radiated from his eyes and in his every action, and whenever Eric came around, Tripp very clearly made a point of marking his territory. Marty loved it. He also loved waking up to Tripp every morning, knowing he wouldn't immediately run for the hills before anyone saw them together.

"Does it involve my favorite morning ritual?" Marty slid a hand over Tripp's hip.

"No."

"No?" Marty huffed. "Then I'm going back to sleep."

Tripp climbed on top of him and pinned his wrists to the bed.

"Mmm . . . I think I might like this idea." Marty rocked his hips upward and purred at the welcome pressure of his erection against Tripp's bare ass.

Tripp's soft lips moved over his, tongue dipping inside and caressing his before retreating along with those fabulous lips. Tripp sat up. "No, I mean I have a plan for my life."

Marty squeezed his eyes shut. "You're killing me here." He tried to shift his thinking to the plan Tripp wanted to share... that didn't involve his dick. But his dick's demands were louder, and he bucked up. He opened his eyes and batted his lashes coquettishly.

"Patience." Tripp laughed and released Marty's wrists, his disapproving frown ignored. "So I was thinking. I might not be able to ride and compete anymore, but I have a lot of experience in this sport. Probably forgotten more than most people will ever learn."

Tripp paused and looked at him expectantly. Marty nodded for him to go on.

"I want to teach bull riding. Professionally. I can probably manage a mechanical bull at slow speed to demonstrate techniques and my own tricks learned over the years. I also want to work with the International Gay Rodeo Association to help promote awareness and tolerance with the PBR and rodeo as a whole."

Warmth spread in Marty's chest, and a smile stretched his lips. Who could have ever guessed what would have happened when Tripp finally faced his fears? Marty had only hoped Tripp would be able to be himself and be happy, but this new Tripp... this incredibly generous cowboy wasn't only fighting for his own happiness, but for the happiness of others as well.

He reached up and ran a finger down Tripp's cheek. "I love you so much."

"Love you too." Tripp leaned down and kissed him quickly. "But I'm not done yet."

"Oh God. There's more?"

"Oh yes!" Tripp bit down on his lower lip. "I was thinking—"

"How about we save the thinking for after?"

"After what?" Tripp made a good attempt at innocent with those big baby blues of his, but Marty wasn't buying it.

"You know." Marty waggled his eyebrows and reached down to take ahold of himself, giving a long, slow tug. "Every good cowboy knows better than to mess with a ritual, lest you anger the gods."

"Listen to you!" Tripp laughed and batted Marty's hand away. Long fingers closed around him, not moving, not squeezing, just... holding. "Plans first, then dick."

Marty flopped back on the bed with a loud sigh. "Torturing me."

Tripp took a deep breath. "We should move in together. We could live here, but I know you'll eventually be taking over the family ranch, so, if it were okay with the rest of the Fairgraves, I could sell this place and move there. With you. Or, we could live here until it's time for you to take over, and then we can see what's the what. Or—"

Marty sat up and pressed his fingers over Tripp's lips, laughing. "I think that's a perfect plan. All of your plans are perfect."

Tripp grabbed his hand and kissed the palm. "Yeah?"

"Yeah. And if you want to move to the ranch with me, then the sooner you get this place on the market the better."

Tripp let out a long sigh and dropped down beside Marty, still holding his cock. He pulled Marty's hand into his and kissed the knuckles. Pride and love swelled inside Marty. Tripp had made so much progress these past months, had gone through so much and come so far. He still had a ways to go, but he was on the right track, and Marty was going to be with him every step of the way.

"Now about your other plan...?"

"Which would that be?" Tripp lifted an eyebrow and sucked Marty's index finger into his mouth, swirling his tongue lazily around it.

Marty rocked his hips, sliding his erection through a tightening grip. "Oh, I think you know."

Tripp smiled. "Yeah. I think that might be one of my better plans."

"Agreed. Now cowboy up."

Acknowledgments

I want to give a big shout out to some amazing people who played a part in helping me bring *Pickup Men* to life. Josh and the MoM critique group for their initial feedback on the first chapters. Rachel and Aleks, for believing in this story enough to take it on. Gordon, for imparting the tools to becoming a better writer, and making me work for it, hardcore. Thorny and Alec, for asking all the right questions, bouncing ideas, and as always, making me smile. M.J. and Taylor, for the word wars, keeping me sane, and getting me through to the end. And finally, Kade, for taking the time to do a 13th-hour read.

ALSO BY
L.C. Chase

Three to Tango, with Chloe Cole

Long Tall Drink

Riding with Heaven

Love Brokers: Mister Romance

ABOUT THE AUTHOR

Artist by day, author by night, L.C. Chase is a hopeless romantic and adventure seeker. After a decade of road tripping on three continents, she now calls the Canadian West Coast home. When not writing tales of beautiful men falling in love, L.C. can be found designing book covers of said beautiful men, reading, drawing, running the trails with her goofy four-legged buddy who, if he were human, would be a stand-up comedian, and fighting her root beer addiction.

You can find L.C. on her website, www.lcchase.com.

Enjoyed this book? Visit RiptidePublishing.com to find more contemporary romance!

Glitterland
ISBN: 978-1-62649-025-3

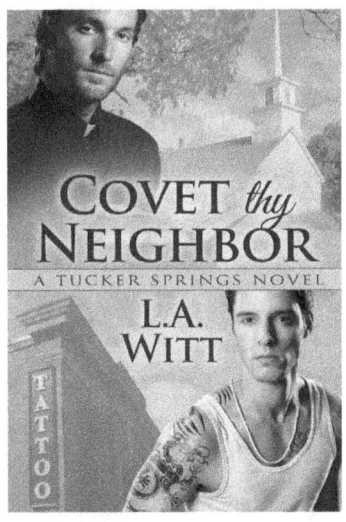

Covet thy Neighbor
ISBN: 978-1-62649-001-7

Earn Bonus Bucks!

Earn 1 Bonus Buck for each dollar you spend. Find out how at RiptidePublishing.com/news/bonus-bucks.

Win Free Ebooks for a Year!

Pre-order coming soon titles directly through our site and you'll receive one entry into a drawing to win free books for a year! Get the details at RiptidePublishing.com/contests.

CPSIA information can be obtained
at www.ICGtesting.com
Printed in the USA
LVHW031507310120
645463LV00002B/317